Piccadilly Press • London

First published in Great Britain in 2012
by Piccadilly Press Ltd,
5 Castle Road, London NW1 8PR
www.piccadillypress.co.uk

A catalogue record for this book is available
from the British Library

ISBN: 978 1 84812 157 7 (paperback)

1 3 5 7 9 10 8 6 4 2

Printed and bound by CPI Group (UK) Ltd, Croydon, CR0 4YY

Cover illustration by Susan Hellard
Cover design by Simon Davis

This, the last in my 21st century Jane Austen series,
is dedicated to my three wonderful, talented
and inspirational daughters,
Niki, Sally and Caroline,
with so much love and pride.

CHAPTER 1

'Nobody meant to be unkind,
but nobody put themselves out of their
way to secure her comfort.'
(Jane Austen, *Mansfield Park*)

'HEY FRANKIE, YOU'VE GOT TO SEE THIS – THIS IS SO YOU!'

'You'd be brilliant in this – get in here quickly!'

Frankie Price hesitated at the foot of the stairs, her finger poised over her iPhone. Her cousins, who had been on a shopping spree, had arrived back half an hour earlier laden with designer-label carrier bags and she could tell from the muffled giggles emanating from the sitting room that this was, in all probability, another wind-up, the kind of teasing that everyone said was 'just a bit of light-hearted fun' but which still hurt far more than she would ever have dreamt of admitting.

'You're made for this, really – come and see!'

So what would it be this time? Frankie wondered.

Mia, twenty-one years old, stunningly beautiful and confident that she was the centre of the universe, showing off yet another lacy mini-dress with the kind of bustier top that looked great on someone with boobs but that would make Frankie look like a rather sad pencil? Or Jemma, eighteen months younger, parading in a skin-tight gold-sequinned jumpsuit and Miu Miu stacks that made her legs look even longer than usual and remarking that it was such a shame that Frankie's shape meant she could never borrow any of their gear?

Frankie sighed, catching sight of herself in the ornate mirror on the opposite wall of the spacious hall. She wasn't ugly, she knew that, but she wasn't beautiful either; she was just five foot three, severely lacking in the boob department, with skin so pale that even an hour in the sun resulted in livid splotches all over her face and arms and a cluster of freckles on the bridge of her rather-too-upturned nose. She yearned to be curvy, she craved straighter hair and luscious lips – but most of all she longed to be bubbly, outgoing and free of the crippling lack of confidence that made her tongue-tied even when her brain was firing out witty – or caustic – remarks in her head.

'Frankie! We know you're out there! Be quick!'

'Busy!' she called, clicking on *Inbox*. She should have heard something by now. They'd said it would be today. Why was the network so slow? She had just turned to head up the stairs, her eyes glued to the iPhone screen, when Mia burst into the hall and grabbed her by the wrist.

'This won't wait,' she insisted, dragging her into the sitting room.

'*Root of the Matter* are looking for people just like you.' If it hadn't been for the acid-tongued presenter, Eleanor Edmonds, holding forth in close-up on the vast plasma TV screen on the wall, Frankie would have assumed she had misheard. *Root of the Matter* wasn't Mia or Jemma's usual viewing choice – it didn't feature celebs locked in some hideously decorated house agonising over their boob enhancements, or fashionistas listing the absolute must-haves in summer tops. It was ITV's most hard-hitting, cutting-edge series, focusing on the social issues of the day and exposing abuse and injustice in everything from care in the community to exploitation of farmers in the developing world.

It was, in fact, the very sort of programme that Ned would have been glued to had he been at home, and for that reason alone, Frankie's curiosity was aroused.

'What do you mean, people like me?' she asked, slipping her phone into the pocket of her shorts. 'What are you on about? Is it a writing competition?'

Ever since she could remember, Frankie had loved writing – not just her diaries but short stories and dozens of letters to magazines and newspapers – she'd even had a couple posted on really prominent websites.

'Better than that – they want teenagers from dysfunctional families to take part in a discussion programme,' Jemma said with mock solemnity.

'And let's face it, families don't come much more dysfunctional than yours, do they?' Mia giggled. 'You've got the lot – lunatic mother, dropout dad.'

'My mum's not a lunatic!' Frankie snapped, knowing

even as she spoke that she should have just turned and left the room. 'She's bipolar. And my dad didn't drop out, he —'

She stopped mid-sentence, aware that she had been about to use all the phrases her father had been prone to use about himself:

'I'm searching for my inner truth, Francesca.'

'I'm a free spirit, Frankie; I can't be hemmed in by the rules and regulations of a blinkered society.'

And, most frequently of all:

'I never expected any of this to happen. It wasn't part of my game plan.'

This last remark would always be accompanied by a series of deep sighs and an expansive gesture meant to include the crumbling house, her mother either weeping buckets or manically joyful depending on the moment, and the pile of unpaid bills that got shoved from table to sideboard and back again without anyone ever making any attempt to do anything about them. As usual, just thinking about her family brought a lump to her throat, rapidly followed by a gut-twisting stab of guilt that she was living in a huge house in one of the most upmarket villages in Northamptonshire while her mum was . . . no, she wouldn't think about where her mum was right now. If she did, she would cry and that was something she only did in the privacy of her own room.

'OK, OK, so he didn't drop out,' Mia scoffed, tossing her copy of *Grazia* magazine to one side and stretching languidly on the sofa. 'He – what's the phrase? *Opted for an alternative lifestyle!*'

'Leave her alone.' Jemma's voice reverted to the softer tones she used when her sister wasn't around and there was no need to keep up with her finely honed cattiness.

'Hey, there you go!' Mia cried. 'There's the website on the screen! Come on, you really should email the programme. It'd be cool – they say they want to see how people survive a bad start in life. They could come here and film us! Because you have to admit, it is down to us that you've got a life at all.'

Frankie took a deep breath, vowing that she wouldn't let their taunts get to her. Over the past couple of years, she had run all manner of scenarios in her head: she had pictured herself coming back with witty retorts when her past was thrown in her face; she had imagined waking up one morning, free of all her stupid inhibitions; she had even set rational thought to one side and imagined her father settling down, buying a house, getting the family back together again and announcing that he was going to care for them all, no matter what. She had made inroads on the first, was working on the second, but even she had to admit that the third was just a childish dream, best forgotten. It was never going to happen.

The fact of the matter was that Mia was right. It *was* down to the Bertrams that she had the sort of life the rest of her family could only dream about. When she had arrived three years earlier, a month after her fifteenth birthday, she had been reeling from what her mother had told her when she had visited her in the psychiatric hospital on her last morning in Brighton.

'You need to know something,' her mother had said, fiddling abstractedly with a strand of prematurely greying hair. 'Your Aunt Tina – the one you're going to stay with – she's not your real aunt. And neither is Nerys.'

She had shuffled in her chair, avoiding Frankie's penetrating gaze.

'You see, I was adopted.'

For a moment, Frankie had thought that her mum was fantasising, that the drugs she took to keep her symptoms at bay were confusing her thinking. Her mother, Ruth, had always referred to Tina (one-time model whose face had graced the covers of *Elle* and *Vogue* and who had married the founder of the hugely successful Bertie's chain of high street clothing stores), and Nerys (wife of Gabriel Lane, rising star in the diplomatic service until he disgraced himself by leaking confidential documents, took to drink and died of alcohol poisoning), as her sisters. On good days, they were the sisters she adored and missed; on bad days, of which there were rather more, they were the smug, self-satisfied so-and-sos of whom she was well rid.

But they were always her sisters.

'So Grandma and Grandpa . . .'

'Weren't your real grandparents, no.' Ruth's voice had flattened and she had stood up and begun pacing the room. 'In fact, I reckon the only reason they upped sticks and moved to Florida was to avoid any risk of ever seeing me – crazy weirdo Ruth – again!'

For some reason she didn't understand, Frankie felt defensive of the not-grandparents who had been been killed in a freeway accident when she was still a toddler.

'I love you, you know that?' Ruth had pleaded, changing the subject as rapidly as she had started it. She hugged Frankie. 'You'll come and see me?'

'Mum, I don't have to go. I can stay with you.'

'And be taken into care? I don't think so.' For just a moment, her mother had sounded more rational than she had for weeks. 'William's got his own life now and I want to know you're safe and being looked after.'

She brushed a tear from her cheek. 'I've failed, Frankie, I've failed you all. I'm useless, worthless . . .'

Frankie hugged her mum tight and waited for the trembling and arm-scratching to pass – just as she had countless times over the years. 'Mum, you're not – you're just not too well right now,' she repeated, almost by rote.

'Yes, you're right, I just need a little rest. And this is an opportunity for you, Frankie,' her mum replied. 'Posh lifestyle in a big house, meeting all the right people, and Nerys says you'll go to a really good school. The teachers always said you were bright but then I was bright once, only life dealt me a cruel blow and now I guess you'll forget I exist . . .'

Frankie had curtailed her mother's increasingly manic outpouring with another hug. 'Mum, of course I won't!' she'd insisted. 'I'll come and see you.'

'You will? Frankie, I love you so much. I never meant it to be like this. I'll get better, I promise I will.'

She smiled bravely and pushed Frankie towards the door.

'Now go – you'll miss your train.'

'Mum . . .'

Frankie couldn't remember which of them had begun sobbing first. She had spent years struggling to care for her mum, manage her schoolwork and deal with the increasingly infrequent and unpredictable visits from her father. She had become adept at pretending to the world that life was totally normal while longing for an escape from it all. But that day, as she'd hugged her mum goodbye, a hole opened in her heart that still hadn't completely closed. Sometimes she wondered whether it ever would.

She would never forget the stomach churning misery of the long journey from Brighton to Northampton, during which she'd discovered that her new mascara, boldly advertised as a hundred per cent waterproof, clearly wasn't, and that the further you get away from the sea the heavier the air becomes. She remembered in sharp detail the anxiety of finding no one waiting as promised on the platform at Castle Station when the train pulled in. She had waited for what seemed like an age, but was probably no more than five minutes, and was just fumbling in her bag for her phone when a large woman in a pleated skirt and maroon gilet had come panting down the steps from the opposite platform.

'Francesca, dear – oh, let me just catch my breath! Ridiculous man at the barrier said you'd be coming in on platform three. Honestly, these days no one knows how to do their job properly! But all's well. Now come along, the car's outside and I don't have all day.'

'Auntie, are we —?'

Nerys had stopped dead in her tracks. 'Oh darling, just call me Nerys! Auntie sounds so pedestrian, don't you think?'

'OK, I —'

'Tina would be the first to agree with me, but of course your Uncle Thomas – well, you'll have to sort that out with him. Not that he's at home right now what with the troubles in Peshawar.'

At the time, Frankie hadn't a clue where Peshawar was or the nature of any troubles except her own, so she had merely kept quiet as Nerys led her to the car park and unlocked the door of her Toureg. As she climbed in, a pungent smell of wet dog assailed her nostrils and two Springer Spaniels began barking and hurling themselves against the protective grille dividing the back seat from the boot. It explained to Frankie why her aunt had smelt so strange on the very infrequent visits she had made to Brighton.

'Quiet!' Nerys shouted and the dogs slumped sulkily down onto the floor as she fired up the engine and rather jerkily reversed out of the parking space.

'Meet Bonnie and Bridie – frightfully well bred but still wet behind the ears. We've got dog training class tonight, however, so that should move things on.'

'Is it far?' Frankie ventured to ask as Nerys swung the car out of the car park, narrowly missing a bollard. She was feeling nauseous and tearful and while her mother had repeatedly told her to 'make intelligent conversation so they know you're just as good as their lot', she was afraid that if she opened her mouth for long she would either throw up or cry.

'Thornton Parslow? Ten miles,' Nerys said, turning onto the dual carriageway. 'Just enough time for me to fill you in on the plans. Of course, it'll all seem very strange to you at first – coming to live with a normal family.'

Frankie's sharp intake of breath alerted Nerys to the tactlessness off her last remark and she reached across and patted Frankie's knee.

'Don't get me wrong, dear, it's not your fault,' she said hastily. 'Your poor mother was always, shall we say, a little strange, even as a child. Blood will out, you know, and rumour has it that her background . . . Well, enough said about that. And then of course, marrying that no-hoper Sean. Sorry, dear, I know he's your father but I said at the time it would end in disaster, and I was right.'

Frankie had been too overwhelmed to comment, not that she would have been able to get a word in edgeways. It didn't take more than ten minutes for her to realise that Nerys Lane loved the sound of her own voice.

'It was me, you know, who suggested you came to live here. Well, after seeing the state of your mother when I popped down to talk with the doctors after that first nasty little episode . . . It was always me that knew my duty to poor Ruth. None of the others made the effort,' she continued, speeding up as they left the town behind them and headed into open country. 'She may have behaved atrociously but as I said to Tina, that's no reason her children should suffer. Oh for goodness' sake, move!'

For a moment, Frankie looked at her in alarm, but realised the last remark was addressed to an elderly man in a rusting Ford Escort who was hogging the outside lane at a sedate thirty miles an hour.

'Honestly, they shouldn't let geriatrics out on busy roads,' Nerys sighed. 'Anyway, where was I? Oh yes – living arrangements. Thomas suggested that you should live with me at Keeper's Cottage, but of course, that was a non-starter. I'm here and there all the time, never a moment to myself: chair of the WI, church warden at St Peter's – we're in an interregnum, you know, and without me the whole place would fall apart – and then there's all my voluntary work not to mention the dog shows: I judge spaniels, you know, very well respected, and —'

There was a sudden jolt as she crashed the gears. 'We turn off here for Thornton Parslow. There are the three Thorntons – Thornton Lacey, Thornton Parva and this one.'

Frankie craned her neck as the car weaved its way down a narrow, twisting lane, dark and shady from the beech and oak trees that formed a canopy over the road. Nerys grabbed her phone from the glove compartment, and with one hand on the steering wheel, punched a button.

'Three minutes away!' she shouted into the phone. 'What, dear? Yes, of course she's all right – we've been chatting.'

Frankie felt that was a slight distortion of the facts

but tried a wan smile as Nerys hurled the handset into the pocket at the side of her seat and beamed at her. 'The family are all ready for you,' she said. 'Much better for you to be at Park House with the girls. You haven't met Jemma and Mia yet, of course – well, not since you were all in nappies! Of course your lifestyles have been so different. I looked up that school you went to on the internet; ghastly looking place, you poor child. Jemma's at Cheltenham, of course, and darling Mia – such a clever girl – has just left and is going to Switzerland to finish.'

Frankie was about to ask what she was going to finish when Nerys stamped on the brakes to allow a pheasant to cross the lane in front of her before hurtling off again. 'Well, here's another surprise: Thomas has managed to get you a place at Thornton College.'

She had turned to look at Frankie, clearly waiting for a cry of delight, and narrowly missed hitting a small boy on a mountain bike.

'Thornton College, dear? One of the top rated schools in the East Midlands? State, of course, but I said to Thomas, private will be too much of a challenge for Francesca, coming from . . . Well, anyway, I'm sure you'll love it.'

When Frankie, swallowing back tears, said nothing, Nerys sniffed and glared at her. 'I hope you'll be grateful,' she said. 'Thornton College is totally oversubscribed but then with Thomas being who he is, it's amazing the doors that open! And of course, they are pledged to take in disadvantaged girls, what with the new government guidelines and everything. Well now, here we are!'

And with that she had pressed a button on the car dashboard, and a pair of wrought-iron gates had slowly opened.

'That's my little pad,' Nerys remarked, as they drove past a small, wisteria-covered cottage. 'It was part of the original estate – it belonged to the gamekeeper in the days when there was shooting in these parts, and, when my husband died, Thomas suggested I took it over. It's much smaller than anything I've been used to but needs must. I struggle financially, but I never complain.'

Frankie didn't know it at the time but Nerys, who had quite enough money to live very comfortably, enjoyed pleading poverty in the same way that her sister Tina enjoyed imagined ill health.

As Nerys had driven the car round the bend in the tree-lined gravel driveway, Frankie caught her first glimpse of Park House. It was grand, far grander than she had expected. Overlooking a huge lawn that led down to a gazebo and tennis court were three storeys of mellow, honey-coloured Northamptonshire marlstone with a huge conservatory to one side and great swathes of Virginia creeper covering the walls. *It's beautiful*, she thought to herself, *but it isn't home*.

Yet now, three years on, it *was* home and she couldn't imagine living anywhere else. For all the teasing from her cousins, she had never once been left out of family events and had been taken to places she had only dreamt of as a child – holidays in Tuscany and Corfu, race meetings and theatre trips to the West End at least three times a year.

At first, whenever she had returned to Brighton to visit her mother, she would deliberately walk past her old home, freshly painted and spruced up by the new owners, and recall the good times before her father had gone and she had been left to cope with her mother's strange moods. And once, after she had been at Park House for eighteen months and her mother seemed so improved as to be moved to a halfway house in Hove, Frankie had imagined them living together in a little cottage near the sea and everything being as it once was. She had been on the verge of mentioning this to Tina when the police had arrived at Park House, and were ushered into the sitting room by an over-important Nerys who just happened to have turned up at the same time. Frankie's mother had been found on Hove esplanade, systematically setting fire to beach huts because she believed her errant husband was sleeping in one of them. Narrowly escaping prison on a plea of diminished responsibility due to forgetting to take her medication, she was sectioned and referred to a secure unit.

She was still there.

'Frankie? Hey, Frankie!' She was jolted out of her reverie by Jemma tapping her on the arm and peering at her anxiously. 'It's OK, we were just having a laugh. Please don't cry.'

'I'm not,' Frankie protested, turning to face her, and then realising that there were indeed a couple of tears trickling down her cheek.

'Yeah, sorry,' Mia murmured, grabbing the remote and idly channel hopping. 'It's not your fault your family are weird.'

'Mia, shut it!' Jemma hissed. 'So . . .' She turned to Frankie. 'What are you going to wear on Saturday, then?'

Frankie frowned, her thoughts still in the past. 'Saturday? What's happening on Saturday?'

'Like, hello?' Mia exclaimed. 'What's the whole civilised world been talking about for the past month? Nick's twenty-first!'

'Oh, that,' Frankie muttered. 'I'm not going.'

'*Not going?*' Jemma gasped. 'What possible reason could you have not to go?'

You want a list? thought Frankie, sighing inwardly. One, Mia's boyfriend was a chinless wonder; two, the place would, she knew, be full of super-confident ex-public-school girls flaunting their perfect figures and talking in over-loud voices about their latest boyfriend, where they've skied and the car Daddy has just bought them; and three, she hated parties. She always had – even the beach parties that all her mates in Brighton had regarded as cool. Sadly, her aunts both considered that it would 'do her good' to socialise at every possible opportunity, and Jemma and Mia, who were so full of confidence in their own charms, kept teasing her and trying to set her up with guys – usually the ones they deemed completely hopeless.

'I'd die to be in your shoes,' her friend Lulu had said a few weeks back when Frankie had shown her the gold embossed invitation card to the party. 'Since my father dragged us to this backwater, I haven't been to one decent party.'

'Nick's will be one of those pretentious affairs where everyone nibbles on canapés and bares their teeth in silly grins till the photographer from *Tatler* leaves and then gets hammered on champagne cocktails and whatever else they happen to have to hand.'

'Sounds good to me!' Lulu laughed. 'Take photos, yeah? I want a snog by snog account of the evening!'

'Even if I go – which I won't – snogging won't feature,' Frankie retorted. 'I'll only know a handful of people anyway.'

'Francesca Price!' Lulu exclaimed. 'Who said you had to *know* someone to snog them? And you have to go. The only way I get a full-on social life these days is by proxy. You owe it to me as my best mate.'

It never failed to surprise Frankie that someone like Lulu – feisty, rebellious and a pain in the neck of practically every tutor at Thornton College – should want to be friends with her, but ever since she had arrived just weeks after Frankie, she had latched onto her and pretty much ignored everyone else.

'Anyway, forget parties,' Lulu had continued. 'You have to promise me one thing, right?'

'What's that?'

'You'll come to all the best gigs at M-Brace? Is it really as great as everyone says it is?'

'I've never been,' Frankie admitted.

'You've never *been*?' Lulu gasped. 'You live practically next door to one of the best music festivals in the whole country and you haven't been? What's that all about?'

'It only happens every other year and last time I was down visiting Mum. Mind you, I don't think my uncle would have been too keen on my being there, judging by the way he yelled at the others for going,' she said. 'He doesn't approve of the festival – says it's a blot on the landscape and ruins the environment.'

'Well, we're going whether he likes it or not,' Lulu said firmly. 'It's the only upside of moving here. And while you're at it, you can make sure you drag that cousin of yours along.'

'Ned?' Frankie felt herself bristle inwardly.

'No, silly, the other one – James. OMG, that guy is so fit!'

Frankie giggled. 'You fancy him!'

'Too right,' Lulu said. 'Has he got a girlfriend at the moment?'

'That's like asking whether a leopard has spots,' Frankie replied. 'He changes them more often than most people change their socks.'

'Great!' Lulu laughed. 'That means he hasn't found the right girl yet. But then again, he hasn't met me!'

Recalling that conversation now, Frankie couldn't help smiling and feeling more than a little envious of her friend's confident, anything-goes nature.

'Hey look, it smiles!' Jemma teased. 'So the thought of Nick's party isn't so horrendous after all?'

'I don't know, I —'

'Honestly, you're hopeless!' Mia sighed. 'I just don't

get why Ned kept on at me to check you'd be there. You're a right party pooper!'

'Ned?' To her annoyance, the word came out as a squeak. 'But he's in Wales.'

'Yes, well, I guess even *he* isn't so saintly that he'd miss out on the kind of party the Rushworths throw just to camp with a load of kids from some inner-city sink estate,' Mia said, zapping the sound on the TV. 'He's done some sort of swap and he's leaving early. He'll be home tomorrow.'

Frankie fought to keep her face expressionless. Ned was the opposite of his twin, Mia; he detested flashy parties as much as Frankie did and no way would he cut short his placement with Kids Out There, or KOT, the charity that was his passion – unless . . .

If he was coming back early, it could surely only mean one thing: he had missed her as much as she had missed him.

'OK, I'll go,' she murmured. 'I guess it would be rude not to.'

CHAPTER 2

'She regarded her cousin as
an example of everything good and great.'
(Jane Austen, *Mansfield Park*)

From: belindap@nenenewspapers.co.uk
To: frankieprice@hotmail.com
Subject: Congratulations!

Dear Frankie,

Congratulations!

I am delighted to inform you that your short story Look Again *has been selected by our panel of judges as the winning entry in our Writers of Tomorrow competition. The judges found your story both imaginative and moving and were particularly impressed by your use of metaphor and irony. As you know, the prize consists of £250 plus free entry for the duration of the M-Brace festival at the end of the month. I would be most grateful if you could telephone me as soon as possible to arrange a time to visit our offices and be photographed receiving your prize.*

Once again, congratulations.

Belinda Painter

Editor, Nene Chronicle

Frankie couldn't stop smiling as she printed off the email. She put it into the box on the top of her wardrobe, along with her private journals and the collection of photographs which her brother William had emailed from the cruise liner *Sea Siren*, on which he was now, as he proudly told her, photographer's assistant to the assistant photographer. It had been a photograph taken with a disposable camera that had won William Best Photo (Portrait) Under Ten in a schools' competition years before and set him on course for what he hoped would be a successful career as a professional photographer. And at last, Frankie felt as if she was finally on the way to fulfilling her dream of being a bestselling author too.

Of course, she admitted to herself, it wasn't just the fact of winning the prize that made her feel as if she was suddenly capable of conquering the universe, it was knowing that Ned was coming home because he wanted to be with her at Nick's party. In many ways, that mattered more than all the writing prizes in the world.

'*Ned.*' She whispered the word into the silence of the room – the same room where he had found her sobbing her heart out a few days after arriving at Park House. She had been angry and mortified – angry that he had burst into the room unannounced, and mortified that this gorgeous eighteen-year-old guy, his white tennis shorts revealing legs to die for, should find her wailing like some stupid kid.

'Oh sorry, I forgot this was your room now!' he had gasped, his face flushing. 'It used to be — Hey, I thought I was the only one who was having a bad day!'

He had squatted down beside her. 'Here – this usually helps. Sorry, I've eaten half of it.' He'd thrust the squashed remains of a bar of chocolate into her hand. 'I guess it must be hard for you, landing here amongst a load of strangers,' he continued, as Frankie struggled to stem her tears. 'I know what I felt like my first term at boarding school, but at least my brother was there. Though come to think of it, that wasn't much help considering he was permanently in trouble and everyone expected me to be a rebel too!'

She rubbed her eyes and glared at him as he burst out laughing. 'What's so funny? You think I'm a baby, right?'

'No,' he assured her, struggling to suppress his laughter. 'It's just that you've now got chocolate all round your eyes! You look like a panda.'

He glanced round her room and snatched a tissue from a box on the dressing table, which he rubbed ineffectually at her eyes.

His fingers touched her cheek and that was the moment when something happened to her heart that she had never experienced before.

'You miss your mum, is that it?' he asked in a gentle tone.

'I miss my brother more,' she admitted. 'He's just got a job on a cruise ship and I promised I'd text him but I've run out of credit.'

'Use mine for now,' he said, tossing his phone into her lap. And just two days later, her uncle had presented her with a brand new phone and promised to pay the bill for as long as her brother was away. She knew that Ned was behind the gift – just as, over the next few weeks, it was Ned who helped her get to grips with the piles of homework from her new school and Ned who alerted his father to the fact that Frankie was the only girl in the class who didn't have her own laptop. He was the one person she could be herself with, the one person who never made her feel small or inferior.

A lot had happened since then but her love for Ned had never wavered. All she needed now was for him to stop thinking of her as some sort of proxy kid sister.

She was about to dial the editor's number when her phone rang and her friend Poppy's name flashed up.

'Hi, Poppy, you OK?' Frankie asked.

'I am so *not* OK as to be KO'd!' Poppy retorted. 'Thanks to my parents, my entire life is in pieces!'

Frankie flopped down onto her bed, kicked off her flip-flops and suppressed a smile. If anyone knew how to make a drama out of a crisis it was Poppy Grant.

'So what's the problem?'

'You won't believe this – Boring Basil's kids are coming to stay.'

'Is that all?'

'Is that ALL? My stepfather's kids are like the most

spoilt, up themselves, pretentious —'

'OK, OK, I get the message,' Frankie chipped in, 'but surely it's not as bad as all that?'

'Not so bad? It's dire,' Poppy ranted on. 'They've had this massive falling out with their mother because she's just shacked up with some guy they don't approve of. Mind you, it is the third time this has happened since she split from my stepdad, so you can see their point. Anyway, they're coming to us tomorrow for the *whole summer* – can you believe it? *Tomorrow*, and my mother's only just told me. And guess what? My stepdad's only gone and given them the granny flat which, if you remember, he promised to me!'

The two Drs Grant, as everyone in the village called them (Poppy's mum being the local GP and her stepfather a research scientist working for one of the big pharmaceutical companies) lived at The Old Parsonage, a large, if somewhat dilapidated Queen Anne house on the other side of the village. Until the previous year, the top floor, once the preserve of servants and governesses, had been lived in by Poppy's grandmother, a feisty woman who had dropped dead at Royal Ascot, due largely to the cumulative effects of a lifetime drinking Martinis and the surge of excitement caused by having just won a sizeable amount of money on a horse coincidentally called Hurry Off.

'I'd got it all worked out,' Poppy went on. 'I was going to go all retro and paint the walls orange with a black ceiling and . . . Oh, it's so unfair. Just because their lives are a mess, why do they have to come and ruin mine?'

For a moment, Frankie said nothing. She had yet to meet Henry and Alice but she suddenly felt sorry for them. She knew only too well what it was like for your life to be a mess, and also to know that despite all the polite welcomes and rehearsed phrases, the people who had to put you up often wanted you anywhere but in their home.

'So anyway,' Poppy went on, 'see you at Nick's on Saturday, yeah? It should be a blast. Have you got your eye on anyone?'

'What do you mean?'

'A guy, silly. Someone you'd like to pull?'

'No one,' Frankie replied, blushing a little as Ned's face flashed across her mind.

'That's good, because my mother's wangled it with Nick's mum to get Henry and Alice invited – so if you're up for grabs, I'll shove Henry in your direction.'

'No way! I thought you said he was a pretentious —'

'He's not that bad,' Poppy reasoned. 'And let's face it, there's no one in your life right now, so you might as well spend the evening with him.' She giggled. 'Besides, I really fancy Charlie Maddox and no way do I want Henry hanging around, cramping my style. He thinks he's God's gift to the female sex.'

Frankie was about to protest when the huge antique gong that Tina kept in the hallway and used as a means of summoning all her various offspring reverberated through the house. Her children told her that it was totally over the top, and ridiculously *Downton Abbey*, but she insisted that shouting to them when she wanted them was not only very common but also bad for her sensitive throat. Tina had a variety of sensitivities and allergies, none of which stopped her from doing what she wanted, but any one of which could be rustled up at a moment's notice if the demands made on her were not to her liking. Since it wasn't lunch or suppertime, Frankie thought something big must have happened.

'Got to go, Poppy,' Frankie said, not without some relief. 'See you later!'

She ended the call, opened her bedroom door and ran down the stairs. As she reached the hallway she saw to her astonishment that it was her uncle who was bashing the gong, his face even more florid than usual, his foot tapping in impatience.

'Uncle!' (Thomas was the one member of the family who refused to be known by his Christian name to anyone under the age of about thirty.) 'I thought you were going to be in London all week.'

Thomas glanced up and beamed at her. This was another surprise: her uncle, while able to smile readily enough when caught on camera watching one of his new lines being paraded at London Fashion Week, was not given to jollity at home. He was a workaholic who, while exceedingly generous to his family and perfectly content for them to do whatever made them happy as long as it didn't involve him, did not view relaxation or leisure time as something that applied to him. To see him not only at home during the week but looking positively cheerful was very odd.

'Francesca!' he cried. 'There you are! Glad you're here – I've something to announce.' He bashed the gong once more. 'Heaven knows where Tina's . . . Ah! Here she comes – oh, and Nerys.'

For a moment his face clouded as Frankie's two aunts (who weren't her aunts) emerged from the kitchen – Tina teetering on four-inch heels and wearing a mini-dress that might have looked vaguely acceptable on someone half her age and Nerys, her trousers covered in dog hairs, striding across the hall and embracing Thomas.

'Thomas, you're home! This is such perfect timing! I've just come up to seek help – I'm having the most awful trouble with my boiler. And the pipes keep making the strangest sound. Of course, I rang the gas people but they're frightfully expensive and I was hoping —'

'Later, Nerys, we'll discuss it later,' Thomas interrupted. 'I have something far more important to tell you all right now.'

Nerys frowned, as if struggling to imagine any issue of more concern to the world at large than the shortage of hot water at Keeper's Cottage.

'You're ill, aren't you?' Tina gasped, snatching her husband's hand. 'You've got something dreadful – I knew it. I told you to go to the doctor when you had that headache last week, and you wouldn't and now you've got us all together to tell us.'

'Tina, I am absolutely fine!' Thomas assured her. 'There is nothing wrong with me – in fact, I've never felt better!'

He flung open the door to the sitting room, where Jemma and Mia were perched on the arms of the sofa, bored expressions on their faces.

'Dad, is this going to take long?' Mia burst out. 'Only

Nick's picking me up in fifteen minutes.'

'Where's James?' her father said, glancing round the room. 'I thought he was due back yesterday.'

'He's at Charlie's,' Mia replied. 'They went out with Nick and everyone last night and got totally hammered and —'

'Mia, you know I detest that sort of language!' her father snapped. 'I sent him a text asking him to be here, saying it was a really big day for me. But I suppose hoping that my eldest child would care is too much to ask.'

For a moment he looked downcast, rather like a small boy who has discovered that Santa Claus is a myth. James was unlike the rest of his family in every way: his brooding, almost Gallic features contrasted with the fair hair and smoky grey eyes of his siblings and his thirst for excitement meant that he spent more time applying himself to any activity that gave him an immediate adrenaline rush than sticking to rules or bothering with passing exams. He was a passionate sailor, a reckless skier and above all, a brilliant musician who played drums for a band that, to quote their own website, 'was going places and fast'. He'd had not one but two gap years before going to uni during which he had kayaked in Africa, sailed round Britain and skied the Lauberhorn twice. He was, in short, the kind of guy that girls adored and adults despaired of – largely because they secretly wished they could have had as misspent a youth themselves.

'That'll be him now,' Frankie said as the heavy oak front door slammed shut. She ran across the room and opened the door, intent on giving James a warning about his father's mood.

'Oh!'

It wasn't James standing in the hall, windswept and suntanned. It was Ned.

'Frankie!'

As he stepped towards her, she caught sight of her reflection in the hall mirror. Scruffy shorts, hair in a mess and a coffee stain on her vest top.

'You weren't meant to be home till tomorrow,' she gasped. *By which time I would have washed my hair, done my face and worn something that made me look marginally older than thirteen*, she added silently.

'I had to get back,' he explained. 'There was no way I could stay once I realised . . . Oh, Frankie, if you knew . . .' He stepped closer and took her hand.

'James? Is that you?' Thomas's voice boomed out from behind the closed sitting-room door.

'No, Dad, it's me, Ned.' The moment was broken as Ned took a deep breath, dropped her hand and walked into the room. Frankie stood stock still, savouring the moment. He was back. And what's more, she was pretty certain what he had been about to say.

'There was no way I could stay once I realised how much I missed you.' Or could it even have been, 'If only you knew how much I love you'? Either way, even winning the writing competition paled into insignificance as she followed him into the room.

'Ned! You're back! This is a bonus!' Thomas cried. 'I wanted you to be here but I didn't think I could drag you away from the adventure camp.'

'Dad, there's something I need to tell you.'

'Later, later,' his father replied. 'No sign of your brother, I suppose.'

'No. Dad, that's what —'

'Oh well, never mind,' his father cried, pulling a sheet of paper from the inside pocket of his jacket and waving it in the air. 'What do you think this is, everyone?'

'A piece of paper,' sighed Mia, raising her eyes to the ceiling.

'Dad, seriously I need —' Ned ventured.

'This,' his father declared, ignoring him, 'is an invitation to Claridges for the Fashion Awards ceremony.'

'Oh, big deal,' Jemma burst out. 'You go every year.'

'Yes, but this time . . .' He paused, beaming at them all. 'I have won the top accolade – Outstanding Achievement in Fashion! What do you think of that?'

'Darling, that's wonderful!' Tina burst out. 'Lovely!'

'Uncle, that's fantastic!' Frankie cried.

'Cool,' Mia murmured.

'Well done, Dad.' Ned's words lacked expression and Frankie noticed that he kept tugging at the collar of his polo shirt, something he always did when he was anxious or distracted.

'And of course,' Thomas went on, 'the timing just couldn't be better with my Cheeky Cheetah adverts hitting TV screens next week.'

'Your new label, of course!' said Nerys. 'I was reading about it in my Sunday paper – such a coup! "Flair and finesse for the front runners of fashion" – that's what Hilary Alexander said.'

'Won't suit you then,' Jemma murmured, winking at Frankie who, drunk on the joys of winning a prize and knowing she was loved by Ned, struggled to suppress her laughter. While Tina made looking glamorous second only to spending hours on her laptop analysing her symptoms and reading up on every new alternative therapy, Nerys had a penchant for corduroy skirts and cable knit sweaters and judged clothing solely as something to keep one warm while walking the dogs or bossing the members of the WI.

'It's going to be a hectic week. *The One Show* have already been onto me, and I'm sure there will be lots of interviews with fashion editors. Suzy Menkes adores my work.'

'So, Dad, well done and all that,' Mia said, jumping to her feet at the sound of a car crunching to a halt on the gravel outside. 'But that'll be Nick, and I have to go, OK?'

She ran to the window and peered out.

'Yeah, it's him – and James is with him. He looks a right mess. Must have been some night he had. Anyway, I'm out of here.' And before anyone could stop her, Mia was out of the door and onto the drive outside.

Ned turned to Frankie and gripped her arm. 'Get to James and stop him making an appearance till I've spoken to Dad,' he hissed in her ear.

'Why? What —?'

'Frankie, just do it, OK? Please.'

The urgency in his voice, and the way he practically shoved her towards the door convinced her that whatever was going on, it was serious.

'Dad, can you come into the conservatory for a moment? There's something you need to —' Ned began as the front door slammed and footsteps thudded across the hall. 'Now, Dad, please!'

The door to the sitting room flew open, almost knocking Frankie off her feet and James, unshaven and with bloodshot eyes, stumbled into the room.

'James, wait! I haven't —' Ned began, but his father pushed him to one side and strode across the room and gripped his elder son by the shoulders.

'OK, I should be angry with you. In fact, I should be incandescent.'

'But you're not?' James asked.

'Well, at least you're here now,' he said, slapping him on the back. 'I was about to suggest we opened a bottle of bubbly.'

'Champagne?' James seemed dumbfounded.

'Oh, of course, you don't know. We've a lot to celebrate.'

'Celebrate?' James glanced at Ned, bewilderment written all over his face.

'Dad's won an award for outstanding achievement in fashion,' Ned said hastily. 'That's what we're all here for.'

'And he doesn't know about . . .?'

'No. Sorry.'

'Well thanks for nothing, Ned!'

James slumped down into the nearest armchair and buried his head in his hands.

'James, what is it? What's happened? Are you ill? Thomas, he's ill!' Tina wailed.

Ned took a deep breath. 'He's not ill,' he said. 'He's in trouble. Real trouble.'

CHAPTER 3

'Thomas though a truly anxious father,
was not outwardly affectionate.'
(Jane Austen, *Mansfield Park*)

'*I've got into a bit of a mess.*'

Frankie's fingers darted over the keyboard. For as long as she kept typing, creating a new story and a wayward hero by the name of Jasper, she could detach herself from the enormity of James's latest escapade. For a character in a story to behave like a complete jerk was one thing; she could manoeuvre the outcome into whatever ending she wanted. Creating a happy-ever-after scenario for James Bertram was going to be a whole lot harder.

'*It wasn't exactly my fault.*'

She highlighted the last sentence and hit *delete*. No way was she going to insult even a fictitious guy by forcing him to spout the garbage with which James had tried – unsuccessfully – to mollify his father. This was one occasion when writing wasn't going to make things any easier to understand.

Who was she kidding? It wasn't what James had done that she was trying to blot out, it was the disappointment of knowing that Ned hadn't come home early to be with her. He'd come because his brother had asked him to.

She pushed back her chair and walked to the window, staring out at the garden. When her uncle had frogmarched James into his study, slamming the sitting-room door behind him with such force that a crack appeared above the lintel, no one had moved, and no one had spoken for a full half-minute. Even Nerys, not known for pregnant pauses, had sat, open-mouthed and wide-eyed, staring into space.

And then from behind the study door the shouting had begun, and as Thomas laid into his son, and James countered each verbal onslaught with more expletives than was probably wise under the circumstances, the rest of the family had started talking, babbling over one another as if trying to blot out the sounds with their own voices.

'I just don't get it. So, like, James stole money?' Jemma had blurted out. (There were a lot of things in life that Jemma didn't get, but on this occasion, Frankie had to admit that she too was at loss to grasp the full horror of it.)

'Surely he didn't actually *steal* it,' Tina had said, her bottom lip trembling as it always did when she hoped to divert attention to her own suffering. 'Maybe he was just stressed and got forgetful?'

She had looked close to tears.

'Tina, don't get upset,' Nerys had said. 'It was probably just a little misunderstanding.'

'A MISUNDERSTANDING?' Ned had exploded. 'James sets up a syndicate with his mates – *mates*, remember? – to buy lottery tickets and then conveniently forgets to buy the tickets and creams off the money for himself.'

'Yes, but —'

'What's more,' Ned had ranted on, 'the odd time their numbers came up, and they thought they'd won ten pounds or even fifty pounds, he persuaded them it was too small an amount to split between thirty of them, so they agreed to plough it back in. And then, as if that wasn't bad enough, he used their money to buy himself essays because he can't be arsed, sorry, *bothered* to do any work. You know he's already had two warnings for plagiarism – well, he's really blown it this time.'

Ned had shaken his head. 'No wonder he's been scared of admitting to anyone that he's been asked to leave uni.' He had sighed. 'It'll break Dad's heart.'

'YOU OWE THEM WHAT?' There was no mistaking the disbelief and fury in Thomas's bellowed demand from across the hallway.

'I guess James has finished the story,' Ned had murmured. 'The bit he avoided mentioning when we were all together.'

All eyes were on Ned.

'There's more?' Frankie had whispered.

'Just this last week, their numbers came up. Between

them they had won ninety thousand pounds.'

'So all's well that ends well,' Tina had said, brightening visibly. 'Lots of money and everyone's happy.'

'No, Mum,' Ned had said, biting his lip. 'James never bought the tickets. So when they all wanted their prize money, he had to admit there wasn't any – and when they asked for their stake money back, he had to confess he'd spent it. What's more, he has debts like you wouldn't believe.'

For a moment no one spoke.

'And now his mates – well, ex-mates by now, I guess – have reported him to the University Dean,' Ned continued. 'He's been sent down, not just for paying other people to write his essays, but for fraud. What worries me is that unless he repays the money in full, I reckon they will hand the whole matter over to the police.'

'Oh no! Rest assured, the police won't be coming near this place.' Thomas, breathing heavily, his forehead beaded with perspiration, had stood in the doorway with James, white as a sheet, behind him.

'Let me make a few things perfectly clear. One, I am going to pay these poor deluded friends of James the money he owes them.'

'Dad! Thank you,' James had said.

'Oh, I'm not doing it for you – I'm doing it because right now the last thing this family needs is a scandal. The more I can do to keep a lid on this the better.'

He gripped the back of one of the sofas for support.

'And of course, I'm thinking of those naive guys you cheated,' he added hastily. 'Rest assured, every penny of that – and the fifteen grand to clear your other debts – will be deducted from your future inheritance.'

'But, Thomas, that's an awful lot of money . . .' Tina began.

'There's no other way,' her husband insisted. 'Damage limitation. Not only am I going to be in the public eye more than ever before, what with the award and the launch of Cheeky Cheetah, but I have a few deals in my sights that could be dead in the water if the family name is tarnished.'

'I might have guessed it would be all about you,' James muttered under his breath. Sadly his father's hearing was more acute than he had bargained for.

'How DARE you!' he exploded. 'It's only through my hard work that the money is available to bail you out in the first place! I started out —'

'With a market stall and thirty pounds in the bank, we know,' James muttered.

Thomas closed his eyes briefly and rubbed his temples. 'And another thing – I'm going on a three-week visit to some of the factories in Mexico on Tuesday, and you're coming with me. You've spent enough time wasting the money I earn – now you can see just what goes in to making it!'

'Dad – no way, I can't,' James spluttered. 'It would mean missing the festival and the band – well, we've got plans.'

'Change them,' his father snapped.

'Dad, I can't!' James protested. 'This festival is our biggest chance so far to make a real name for the band. The organisers said our demo tape was ground breaking and they've given us a slot for the ENT evening!'

'Ear, nose and throat?' Tina frowned.

'Emerging new talent,' James snapped.

'If you had been less obsessed with bands and a playboy lifestyle, you wouldn't be in this mess!' Thomas shouted. 'Maybe knuckling down to work with me will make you see sense.'

James bit down hard on his lip and turned away. Frankie could see that he was actually fighting back tears and for a moment, despite his stupidity, she felt sorry for him. Music was his life; Frankie was well aware that despite Thomas's hopes and dreams of his son following him into the business, all James wanted was to be a professional musician.

Thomas turned to the rest of the family. 'And none of you will breathe a word of this to anyone outside this room,' he went on. 'On Saturday we will all be at the Rushworths' for Nick's party – the Grants will be there, the Peabodys . . . people whose respect I cannot afford to lose and —' He stopped short. 'Mia! She doesn't know about this. Right! We'll keep it that way. Get the party done with and tell her then; I don't want her blabbing to Nick's parents – not yet. They're planning to invest some more cash in an idea of mine and, well, let's just say the timing of all this couldn't be worse.'

'Dad, Mia has a right to know what's going on,' Jemma said. 'You can't just leave her out.'

'Leave her out? You talk as if I am depriving her of a trip to the opera!' Her father snorted. 'For the time being, the story is this: James failed his exams and has only just owned up. The subject is now closed.'

'Ned? Are you OK?'

Unable to forget the look of misery on Ned's face after his father had slammed the door shut and headed off down the drive in his new Porsche, and desperate to share her news, Frankie had spent half an hour searching for him. She also wanted to make sure he hadn't forgotten that he'd promised to take her out for driving practice in Tina's hatchback as soon as he got home. With her test only a couple of weeks away, she needed all the practice she could get.

She found him slumped in one of the faded wicker chairs in the summerhouse at the far end of the garden, headphones in his ears. Seeing her, he switched his iPod off and managed a half-hearted smile. 'I just needed some space,' he said by way of explanation. 'I feel so guilty.'

'*Guilty?* What have you got to feel guilty about? None of that mess was your fault.'

Ned sighed. 'No, but James will be swanning off to Mexico, debts all cleared and his life pretty much as it's always been.'

'He's been chucked out of uni, and your dad's really mad with him.'

'Like James really cares,' Ned said, with more bitterness in his voice than she had ever heard before.

'All he wants to do is music anyway. But thanks to him, all my plans have been scuppered before they started. And I feel guilty for caring so much.'

Frankie sat down on the floor beside him and frowned. 'What do you mean?'

Ned glanced down at her, then put his head in his hands. 'This mustn't go any further,' he said eventually, 'but I have to talk to someone and you're the only one who might just possibly get it.'

'Go on.'

Ned stood up and began to pace up and down on the bare floorboards. 'I'd been meaning to tell Dad that I wanted to switch courses at uni,' he confessed. 'I'd steeled myself for the row that I knew would follow but I was – I *am* – so sure it's the right thing for me that I felt he would come round to it in the end. But now —'

'Hang on,' Frankie butted in. 'Just because James has messed up, it doesn't mean you can't do what you want.'

'But don't you see, it does!' Ned sighed. 'If I start a new course now, Dad'll hit the roof; you know what a stickler he is for "seeing things through to the end" and all that. Plus I'll have to get a student loan because no way will Dad fund me when he hears what it is I want to do.' He shook his head and sighed. 'I guess I'll just have to knuckle down, to use Dad's phrase, and finish the course.' He picked up his iPod and walked towards the door.

'No, wait!' Frankie grabbed his arm. 'You told me that if you have a dream and don't follow it, that's like wasting a God-given opportunity, remember? When everyone was saying I should spend less time writing and more time working on my maths and science, you said —'

'That's different, Frankie.'

'No it's not! I listened to you and because of that I've won the competition and —'

She stopped in mid-sentence, never having intended to blurt out her news like that.

'Won? The Writers of Tomorrow thing? Frankie, why didn't you say? There was me going on and on about my own stuff and – oh, this is wonderful!'

He grabbed her, gave her a bear hug and spun her round till she felt dizzy.

'Stop it!' She laughed in delight. 'I've just phoned them. I've got to go and have my photo taken receiving the prize.'

'Cool – what have you won?'

'I'll tell you later. But stop trying to change the subject,' she said. 'What do you really want to do?'

'You won't laugh?'

'Have I ever?'

'OK.' He nodded, jumping down the steps from the summerhouse onto the flagstone path. 'I want to be a social worker. I've thought about it for months, and this last couple of weeks with the kids from Bradford – well, it just made me all the more sure this is what I was meant to do.'

'Won't the degree you're already doing be enough?'

'I'd still have to do loads more training and anyway – oh, Frankie, I hate it! If I had known how deadly dull business and management was I would never have enrolled. The more I study, the more I realise it's just not me. I'm not interested in takeovers and market share and all that stuff. I want to work with kids.'

'Like the ones that you took to camp?' Frankie asked.

'Yes! Making a difference for kids who've had a lousy start in life is a lot more important than marketing next season's must-have coat! That's what I want to do – make a difference.'

For the first time that day his face lit up, his features came alive and his words were filled with passion.

'When you talk like that, I love you even more – oh! I mean, I love to hear all about your plans. You should go for it.'

She bent down and feigned huge interest in a snail on the path as she felt the colour rush to her cheeks.

'You really think so?' To her relief Ned appeared not to have noticed her near blunder. 'I wouldn't have to leave Durham – they do a BA in social work and I've been checking it out with some guys who are on it and it's just amazing! Frankie, it's just so what I dream of doing.' His face suddenly clouded. 'But Dad . . . Now there's all this trouble with James . . .'

Frankie touched his arm. 'I know it's really good of him to clear the debt, but let's face it, he does have loads of money.'

'Not half as much as you'd think by the way we live,' Ned sighed. 'Most of it gets reinvested so he can expand his empire – and anyway, it's not really about the money. He's so set on one of us getting involved in the business and since it's not going to be James, and the girls have made it abundantly clear that they'd rather have root canal work, he'll be focusing all his hopes on me.' He bit his lip. 'But you're right. I should bite the bullet and talk to him. Not yet though. Not till he's back from Mexico. If everything goes well out there, and if he gets loads of positive publicity from this award, he's bound to be in a better mood.'

He put a hand on Frankie's shoulder. 'Thank you,' he said, touching her cheek. 'What would I do without you?'

Frankie's heart lifted and she held her breath as he turned to face her.

'You're a better sister to me than either of my real ones. Which reminds me – you are coming to Nick's party, aren't you?'

Frankie nodded, swallowing her disappointment that the hoped-for kiss hadn't been forthcoming.

'And you're still mates with Poppy Grant, right?'

'Sure – why?'

'Well, there's this girl. I met her briefly a few weeks back at a party that James dragged me along to because the band was playing there. She was lovely. Anyway, you won't believe this, but it turned out she's Poppy's stepsister and she just sent me a text to say that she's coming to —'

'To stay with the Grants, her and her brother.'

'You know? Poppy told you?'

'Yes,' Frankie replied flatly. 'And yes, they're going to Nick's on Saturday.'

Fate, she thought, could be very cruel.

'That's great, because then you can find out just how things stand with Alice. You know, whether she's got anybody or not. It'll come better from you. I don't want to make a fool of myself by coming on strong and then finding she's in a relationship.'

'You don't need me, you could always just ask Poppy,' she countered curtly, her heart sinking for the third time that day. She kept her eyes focused on the ground, fearing that if she looked up at him he'd see her tears.

'What?' Ned laughed. 'And have it round the entire county that I fancy Alice Crawford? I don't think so. You I can trust. Now come on, let me see this prize-winning story. I can't wait to read it.'

'Later.' Frankie managed to stifle a sob as she turned go inside the house. 'I'm not in the mood right now.'

CHAPTER 4

'Family squabbling
is the greatest evil of all . . .'
(Jane Austen, *Mansfield Park*)

FRANKIE WOKE ON SATURDAY MORNING TO THE SOUND OF doors slamming and voices raised.

'You can't boss me about like this, Dad! I'm twenty-two for God's sake,' James was yelling.

'With the social conscience of a six year old,' his father stormed. 'Now for the last time, pack a case and be downstairs in half an hour. Or consider yourself responsible for your own debts.'

Frankie glanced at her bedside clock. It was only six-fifteen; something serious must have happened for her uncle to be up this early on a Saturday. Shrugging her arms into her bathrobe, she opened the door and ventured downstairs.

From the kitchen she could hear Tina in full flood.

'Thomas, you can't go to Mexico now – what about the award? The press will be phoning.'

'And I'll talk to them – that's what iPhones were invented for,' he replied sarcastically. 'Just make sure you pick up all today's newspapers and all of Sunday's too, OK?'

'Yes, but what about the Rushworths' party tonight? I can't go on my own.'

'Don't be ridiculous, of course you can. The kids will be there, Nerys is going – you don't need me.'

'What will people think? You're Nick's godfather! And besides, you promised to drive me to London on Monday to see my new therapist.'

'Tina, can't you get it into your head that the manufacture of my entire range of next spring's Zeppelin label is rather more important than a visit to a quack waving a few crystals over your stomach,' Thomas replied wearily. 'The trouble in Tehuacan has worsened over the past twenty-four hours and I need to get there asap.'

Frankie was heading back to her room, having decided that keeping out of the way was the safest option, when Jemma appeared at the top of the stairs, rubbing her eyes and yawning. 'What's going on?'

'Your dad has to go to Mexico right away,' Frankie said.

'*What?* Like today? He so can't do that.' Suddenly she appeared wide awake, a look of genuine horror on her face.

'Judging by the suitcase in the hall, he can and he is,' Frankie replied.

'Don't see why you're surprised, Jem – surely you know by now that our dear father always does what he wants when he wants.' James chucked a holdall out of his bedroom door and kicked it viciously across the landing.

'He's just bailed you out,' Frankie reasoned. 'He didn't have to do that.'

'He did it to save his own face.' James shut his bedroom door and gave the holdall another, rather more feeble, kick. 'But yes, I'm sorry. I know I've been an idiot and of course I'm grateful. It's just that I'm gutted to miss the festival – I feel like I've let the other guys down big time.' He rubbed a hand over his eyes. 'We've worked so hard to get this far with the band, and so much hangs on this ENT gig. Besides, I've no interest in going to Mexico, or anywhere else remotely connected with his business for that matter.'

'James? James! The taxi's here. Get down now!' Thomas stood at the foot of the stairs, glaring at his son.

'Dad, you can't go today – can't it wait till after the weekend?' Jemma cried, her mules flapping on the stairs as she ran towards him. 'Tonight's really important.'

'When will this family get it into their heads that nothing – I repeat, *nothing* – is more important than making a success of the business? *Nothing*.'

'And that,' muttered James as he picked up his holdall and stomped down the stairs, 'says it all.'

Are you there? Have you pulled someone? I need details – now! Lulu xx

Yes. No. Later. Frankie smiled to herself as she hit

send knowing that her reply would make Lulu even more impatient. She might have been tempted to say more – how Southerton Grange made the Bertrams' seven-bedroomed house look like a country cottage and how there appeared to be a contest between all the girls at the party as to who could show the most cleavage – but right now she had more important things to focus on than satisfying Lulu's appetite for gossip.

When they had first arrived, later than they intended after fielding phone calls from newspaper and TV editors who couldn't reach Thomas on his mobile ('He's in midair en route to Mexico,' Ned had told them repeatedly), she had been so overwhelmed by the sheer over-the-top extravagance of the spectacle that Nick's doting parents had laid on for their only son's twenty-first birthday that all thoughts of Ned's reason for being there in the first place were temporarily forgotten.

'However much must all this have cost?' she had murmured to Ned, gazing at the lavishly decorated entrance hall, complete with palm trees, fairy lights and an old-fashioned barrel organ; at the mini funfair in the front garden complete with coconut shies and a carousel and, spotted through the floor to ceiling windows of the dining room, the tables groaning with food, ice sculptures and three chocolate fountains (which Jemma, who was doing a catering course, assured her were very last year and bordering on chavvy).

'Enough to fund at least a dozen kids to go on an adventure camp for a week,' Ned had muttered back. 'The Rushworths never did do understated. But we're here, so we might as well enjoy it.'

Entering the huge drawing room, Frankie felt all the old shyness and insecurity flood back. While Jemma and Ned seemed perfectly at ease with the air kissing and 'Darling, how lovely to see you again's, Frankie was acutely conscious that she was only there because it would have been rude to leave her out. Verity Rushworth, a large (the upper classes are never described as obese) woman with pudgy fingers adorned with huge diamonds, said all the right things but made no eye contact. Her husband, Seamus, who wore the expression of a man who knows that the six hours stretching ahead of him will cost three times as much as he imagined, called her Freya and squeezed her hand too hard and for too long. As for Nick, the birthday boy onto whose arm Mia was clinging like a limpet in a rough sea, he looked as he always did – like an overexcited ten year old who has found himself in the middle of Disneyland and doesn't know where to start having fun first.

Frankie knew before he opened his mouth what he would say.

'Hello, Frankie – some do this, isn't it? The parents have really gone to town. Well, not actually to town of course, because they're here but . . .'

She smiled wanly, wished him a very happy birthday and, not for the first time, wondered how it was that someone could be on the planet for twenty-one years and still be so vacuous.

It was as they made their way through the double doors into the vast open-sided marquee in the back garden, that Frankie became conscious of Ned's eyes scanning the clusters of guests who were sipping their Bellinis and trying to look as if they weren't desperate to catch the attention of the photographer.

'I can't see . . .' he began, but broke off as Mia and Nick, arm in arm, came over to them.

'Hey, Ned, where's Dad? We've been looking for him everywhere.'

'Ah,' Ned said. 'I guess you haven't heard then.'

Mia had stayed overnight at the Rushworths, putting her event management course to good use.

'He had an emergency call,' Ned explained and filled her in on the details.

'What? You mean he's not coming? That'll ruin everything.' Mia looked genuinely crestfallen.

'No it won't, babe,' Nick assured her, giving her shoulder a squeeze. 'Tell you what.' He leant forward and began whispering in her ear.

'OK, then!' Mia brightened visibly. 'Ned, over here! We need to tell you something.'

'Can't it wait?' Ned replied, his eyes still scanning the room.

'It so can't,' Mia said, a grin like a Cheshire cat's spreading across her face.

'Major urgency, no can put on hold!' Nick cried. 'Whole evening hangs on this moment! Follow me!'

With that, Nick strode through the marquee and out into the garden, Mia clinging devotedly to his arm – although it did occur to Frankie that she might simply be using him for support as her five-inch heels struggled to cope with the coconut matting.

Ned sighed. 'That guy gets more stupid by the day. I just don't get what Mia sees in him. But then again, I guess when you're the sole heir to the Rushworth jewellery empire, it's not your brain that girls notice.'

He took Frankie's hand, causing her heart to miss several beats, and led her further into the marquee. 'There's Poppy,' he said eagerly, gesturing to the far side of the big tent. 'I'll go and listen to whatever nonsense Nick has to tell me, and you find out whether Alice is here. OK?'

'Of course,' Frankie muttered. *And if she is, I might be seriously tempted to throttle her*, she thought as she made her way past a couple of giggling girls and a guy who looked the spitting image of Robert Pattinson in one of his less believable roles.

'Frankie! At last! I thought you'd never get here!' Poppy sashayed over to her and slipped an arm through hers. 'Is this cool or what? I've had three Bellinis already.'

'I guessed,' Frankie teased. 'Listen, Alice and Henry – are they here?'

'Aha!' Poppy cried. 'So you *do* like my plan after all! I told you that being on your own was overrated. I'll get Henry – he's yabbering on at Charlie.'

'No,' Frankie said. 'It's Alice I'm looking for. Ned thinks he knows her.'

'Really? That's so random! Come on, she's over here, probably telling everyone how wonderful she is. I'll introduce you.'

She dragged Frankie across the room towards a group

of guys who were clearly vying for Alice's attention.

'Hey, Alice.'

She's stunning, Frankie thought, her heart sinking as Poppy called to a tall, slender girl with flawless skin and hair so glossy that it could have been digitally enhanced. Poppy had mentioned that Alice was doing fashion studies at uni and it showed. She was wearing a pure white dress with shoulder straps and in her hair she wore a single pure-white gardenia and even her eyebrows, which were pencil thin, were studded with tiny stick-on sequins.

'Perfect timing,' Alice whispered to Poppy, smiling to show perfectly even, whiter than white teeth. 'When guys start spouting chat-up lines straight from comic strips, I'm so out of here.'

She began to move away.

'Alice, wait, I want you to meet Frankie,' Poppy said. 'She's a mate of mine and she's a cousin of Mia Bertram, Nick's girlfriend. I told you about the Bertrams, right?'

'You did!' Alice nodded, scanning Frankie from head to toe and then fixing a fake smile on her lips. 'Tennis court, big paddock, bossy aunt and the chance of some discounted designer gear if I play my cards right?'

'Alice! I didn't say . . .'

'OK, so I added that last bit myself!' Alice laughed. 'But you know what? I've been trying to remember where I'd heard the name Bertram before, and it's just come to me! I met this rather sweet guy at a party.'

'That'll be Ned,' Frankie replied stiffly. 'He's around here somewhere.'

'Ned?' Alice frowned. 'That might be the one, although I'm not sure – I meet so many guys that I get muddled over names.'

'Get *you*!' Poppy retorted, voicing precisely what Frankie had been thinking.

'Oh, I didn't mean it to come out like that,' Alice said hastily, the silver bracelet on her right wrist glinting as she held her hand up in mock horror. 'Truly, I meant – well you know what boys are like. They see a girl on her own and they think they're in.'

'Mmm,' Poppy mused. 'I wouldn't know. I'm so rarely on my own.'

Nice one, thought Frankie, as Poppy gave a breezy wave and sauntered across the room, picking up another Bellini from a waiter on the way.

'So, Frankie,' Alice said, 'give me the lowdown on some of the guys around here. Poppy says I have to keep my hands off Charlie Maddox but having met him for ten seconds when we arrived, she's got nothing to worry about there. Definitely not my type.'

'What *is* your type?' Frankie asked, trying to sound laidback and disinterested.

'Clever, ambitious, witty and rich.' She laughed. 'Although I have been known to accept three out of four if the guy is really fit. So are you with anyone?'

'Hopefully not.' The guy who had spoken was so like Alice – the same dark hair, blue-green eyes and identical aquiline nose – that it didn't take a genius to work out that this was Henry, and Frankie found herself instinctively taking a step back as he positioned himself firmly between her and his sister.

'This,' Alice confirmed, 'is my twin brother Henry. He doesn't want to be here and he'll probably be in a foul mood all evening.'

'I *didn't* want to be here,' Henry said, raising an eyebrow at Frankie, 'but that was before Poppy pointed you out to me. That's when everything changed.'

Oh yuck, Frankie thought. *As come-ons go that ranks with a Year Seven's worst attempts*.

'Poppy says you're a writer and a prize-winning one at that,' Henry went on. 'I'd love to read your stuff. Give me your blog address.'

'But I don't —'

'Why not?' Henry interrupted.

'I did think about it,' she admitted. 'My brother has one – he posts his photographs and —'

'LADIES AND GENTLEMEN, YOUR ATTENTION PLEASE!'

The Master of Ceremonies, in a red tailcoat and white waistcoat, mounted the podium at the top end of the marquee and banged his gavel on the table.

'Oh God, I do hope this isn't going to be horribly formal.' Alice sighed. 'I do so hate these all-age dos – I reckon grannies and aunties should stay at home out of the way and let those of us who know how to really party get on with it!'

'If it was my party, I'd want all my family to be around,' Frankie replied. 'No matter what.'

'Really? That's so sweet, especially considering,' Alice replied.

Frankie felt cold suddenly. 'Considering what?'

'I mean, Poppy mentioned that you come from a broken home and that your mother's had all sorts of problems and your dad's a total —'

'Poppy talks too much,' Frankie replied through clenched teeth.

'BEFORE SUPPER IS SERVED, SILENCE FOR MR NICHOLAS RUSHWORTH!'

'Speeches? Now?' Alice muttered. 'How boring!'

The MC stepped back as, to a burst of applause, Nick, holding Mia firmly by the hand, stepped onto the podium, stumbled and fell flat on his face.

The MC smiled – he obviously knew Nick well. 'Drunk already, Mr Rushworth?' he joked. 'Never could hold his drink! Up, up up!'

Amid raucous laughter and slow handclaps, Nick staggered to his feet, beaming and apparently taking all the banter in good part. He held up his hand and the room fell silent.

'Laugh all you like, but I had good cause to be knocked off my feet because, well . . . the thing is – you'll all be surprised – *I* was surprised —'

'Get on with it, mate!' someone shouted.

Nick turned to Mia who was nodding encouragingly. 'Half an hour ago I asked Mia to marry me and she said yes! We're engaged!'

Amid an outburst of cheers, applause, gasps and hugs, Mia flashed a huge diamond ring at the photographer.

'Engaged?' Alice gasped. 'She only looks about eighteen.'

'She's twenty-one,' Frankie said, hardly able to believe what she'd just heard. 'And they've been going out since way before I knew them. Wow!'

'But to think about getting married . . .' Alice shook her head.

'What a waste!' Henry said, gawping at Mia with a look of disbelief on his face. 'Why would anyone in their right mind even think about getting married at our age?' He turned to Frankie. 'Getting tied down is so – primitive! At any age, come to think of it. Don't you agree?'

Frankie was about to reply when Jemma dashed up to her and grabbed her by the arm, a huge smile on her face.

'I knew he was going to propose to her! I knew all about it but Nick swore me to secrecy. He borrowed my finger last week to get the ring size right! That's why I tried to stop Dad going away.' She glanced at her sister, who was pouting coyly for the camera. 'Isn't it so romantic? They're going to move in together – Nick's parents are buying them an apartment in Brighton and —'

'In Brighton? Their own flat?' Frankie gasped. 'Just like that?'

Despite having moved in these circles for three years, there were still times when the way the other half lived took her breath away. She knew the Rushworths were rolling in money and that they doted on their only son but still – a flat all of their own?

'Oh come on, everyone knew it would happen

sooner or later,' Jemma said. 'They've been going out for seven years and you know Mia – she always said she couldn't imagine being with anyone else. And as for the apartment, it makes sense because Nick's doing viti . . . viti . . . that studying wine growing thing at Plumpton.'

'Viticulture,' Frankie murmured.

'And when Mia's finished her event management stuff at Brighton Uni she's got a placement at the Hotel du Vin,' Jemma said. 'Lucky sods.' For a moment, she looked downcast. 'It's not fair – Mia's getting married and she's getting a flat, James gets all his debts paid off just to hush up —'

'Jemma, this is Alice Crawford, Poppy's stepsister, and her brother Henry,' Frankie interrupted hastily, pulling a face at Jemma and talking more loudly than she would have liked to override any faux pas Jemma was about to make. 'This is Jemma, Mia's sister.'

'Hi,' Jemma said casually and then focusing on Henry murmured, 'Well, hi!' in what Frankie could only imagine she thought was a sexy voice but which actually made her sound as if she was coming down with a severe case of tonsillitis.

'I reckon we should go and congratulate the birthday boy and the bride to be,' Alice remarked, clearly bored. 'Come on, Henry.'

'I'll be back,' Henry whispered to Frankie. 'You are without doubt the only interesting person I've met here so far!'

He winked at her and followed his sister through the

crowd of giggling guests thronging around Nick and Mia, Jemma hot on their heels.

Frankie would have followed them, had she not seen Ned heading her way.

'You let her go?' There was no mistaking the note of accusation in Ned's voice. 'Did you tell her I was here? Did she remember me?'

'Yes, she remembers you,' Frankie replied, hoping that the irritation and sadness she felt didn't show on her face. 'She's over there, congratulating Mia, if you want to catch her.'

'Did you have any idea about Mia and Nick?' he asked, pushing his way past clusters of guests in the direction of the dining room as Frankie struggled to keep pace.

'Not a clue. To be honest, I don't get what she sees in Nick.'

'A villa in Barbados, apartment in Klosters and pied-a-terre just off the King's Road, I imagine!' Ned replied sarcastically. 'I sometimes wonder whether I come from the same gene pool as the rest of my family. Anyway, I sent Dad a photo of Mia and Nick looking like the worst kind of magazine cover.'

Frankie laughed. 'What does your mum say?'

'She's all over the place – furious that she wasn't told first and excited at the thought of being mother of the bride! At least it's stopped her talking nonstop about Dad's award!' He took her hand as they approached the dining room. 'Shall we go into supper?'

Frankie's spirits lifted – Ned wanted to sit next to her! 'Sure.' She was determined not to sound over keen.

'Great – because I'm hoping we can fiddle the seating plan so I get to be near Alice. I have a feeling she might be the one good thing about this evening.'

As promised, an update on evening from hell: Mia's engaged to Nick R! Ned drooling over sickeningly pretty girl called Alice. Jemma's coming on strong to Henry and I'm sitting in the loo cos it's better than dancing with guys with 2 left feet and a total lack of deodorant. Talk tomorrow? Got amazing news but you'll have to wait till I can see your face! xx

Frankie had sent her text to Lulu and was about to open the cubicle door of the Portaloos in the back garden when there was a clatter of heels and the sound of a familiar voice.

'You don't waste much time, do you? And Ned Bertram of all people!' Poppy's voice was slightly slurred.

Frankie bristled, then stood motionless, straining to catch the rest of the conversation.

'What do you mean "of all people"?' Alice replied. 'I'm bored, and he's up for grabs. He said there wasn't anyone in his life right now.'

Frankie felt a lump rise in her throat as the door to the adjacent cubicle slammed shut and the bolt slid across.

'And more to the point, he's going to ask his father if I can use their paddock.'

'To pitch a tent? Oh great – I get the granny flat back,' Poppy retorted sarcastically.

'No, idiot,' Alice countered. 'For Fling.'

'Your horse? I thought you were leaving him down in Sussex with your mum.'

'Oh, the new man has just decided it's too expensive to keep Fling at livery,' Alice replied. 'Tight-fisted old . . .'

And then Frankie could hear no more over the noise of the loo flushing. When the sound subsided, it was Poppy who was speaking.

'Anyway, you should watch out, because I reckon Frankie's got a thing going for Ned.'

'Well, all's fair in love and war and – be honest. She's sweet, but hardly a live wire, is she? Though Henry seemed to think she was worth pursuing. But then again, you know Henry!'

'Sadly, I do,' Poppy muttered and Frankie almost laughed.

'Anyway,' Alice continued, 'now that Ned's agreed to teach me to drive in exchange for me teaching him to ride, we're going to be seeing a lot of one another. Hey, that's the fireworks starting – let's go!'

Frankie didn't move. A vision of Ned cantering in slow motion with Alice at his side made her feel slightly sick.

There is, however, only so long one can sit in a cramped cubicle, especially when people are queuing outside. She had never been very keen on fireworks and instead of hovering on the edge of the crowd of partygoers, all ooh-ing and aah-ing at the explosions of colour shooting and spiralling into the night sky, she turned towards the house and was about to go in when she saw Henry leaning against the wall and heard the sound of giggling.

'I mean it. You being taken – it's a tragedy.' Henry's voice was deep and gravelly.

More laughter.

'You're crazy, you don't even know me.' It was as she thought. Mia's voice was unmistakable. Frankie stiffened and slipped behind one of the huge stone urns spilling over with aquilegia and fuchsias. She strained to catch their words above the bangs and swishes of the fireworks.

'All I'm saying is that I wish I had met you a month ago,' she heard Henry say. 'Mia, you are without doubt the only interesting person I've met here. In fact, the moment I saw you this evening something happened to me that has never happened before.'

Urgh! He even uses the same chat-up lines, Frankie thought.

'Clearly this something wasn't engaging your brain,' Mia replied coyly. 'I'm engaged to Nick.'

'Do you love him?'

'Of course I do – not that it's any of your business.'

'Does your heart race every time you see him? Is every day with him exciting and fun? . . . No, I didn't think so.'

'I am so not standing around to listen to this!' Mia said. 'Who do you think you are?'

'I think,' he said pulling Mia towards him and running his hands over her backside, 'that I am the kind of guy who could show you a good time and . . .'

A rocket exploded followed by a volley of firecrackers, temporarily blotting out his words.

'Get lost!'

Frankie sighed with relief as she saw Mia push him away and stumble somewhat drunkenly down the terrace steps, calling Nick's name. Suddenly she stopped and turned round. 'What kind of good time?' she called, and then disappeared into the crowd.

She heard Henry give a low chuckle and saw him saunter into the house.

'Oh babe,' Frankie heard him murmur under his breath, 'the fun is only just beginning.'

CHAPTER 5

'A compliment?
Heavens rejoice, she complimented me!'
(Jane Austen, *Mansfield Park*)

'I NEVER THOUGHT I'D BE SO GLAD TO SPEND A DAY IN Northampton in my whole life,' Frankie said, as the bus pulled away from the village the following Wednesday morning. 'The last few days have been beyond belief.' She smiled at Lulu. 'And it's really sweet of you to come with me,' she added. 'Do I look OK? I mean, kind of professional but not over the top?'

'You look great,' Lulu assured her. 'Anyway, you're meeting the editor of a regional daily, not the chairman of the BBC! So come on, fill me in on what's been going on. Sorry about not meeting up on Sunday. Honestly, of all times for my parents to decide we should dash off after church to visit Granny and Grandpa – just as life up here is getting interesting!'

'I don't know where to start,' Frankie admitted.

'So far I'm up to the end of the party,' Lulu said, 'and James going to Mexico and missing it all, which on the one hand is cool because he won't have met anyone new, but on the other is the total pits because if he's going to be away for the festival, I won't get a chance to pull him!'

'You're outrageous!' Frankie laughed.

'Well, if *you* were a bit more outrageous, you just might make more progress with Ned,' Lulu replied pointedly. 'Anyway, enough about my disastrous love life. You said something happened on Sunday?'

Frankie thought back to what had happened.

'So you've surfaced at last,' she'd teased, as Ned appeared at the kitchen door on Sunday morning. 'Finally slept off the effects of last night then?'

'I've been up ages,' he had replied. 'I wanted to talk to Dad and I had to work out the time difference. Guess what? He said yes!'

'I guess he couldn't really say no,' Frankie reasoned. 'They're both over eighteen and —'

'Not about the engagement,' Ned said. 'Nick had already won him over by phoning before he asked Mia. No, I mean he was cool about Alice using our field and paddock to graze her horse. What's more, I'm going to clean out the old stable so she can use that too. I can't wait to tell her. I'm off to the Grants now.'

'Can't you just ring her?'

'Well I could, but I wanted to see her face when she

heard the news. Besides, I thought now was as good a time as any for her to have her first driving lesson. Well, not her first ever, but her first with me.'

'Oh.' Jealousy had gnawed at Frankie's stomach with an intensity that took her by surprise. 'I thought . . . I mean you did say you'd take *me* out driving before lunch.'

'Did I? Oh, so I did. Sorry. Still, we can do it any time, can't we? This afternoon – we'll go then. It'll be a good excuse to escape because Verity Rushworth is coming over to talk engagement announcements and photos in *Country Life* with Mum!'

'And . . .' she'd hesitated.

'What?' Frankie detected a faint note of impatience in his voice.

'Nothing.'

'No, go on. Do you need me for something else?'

Yes, but I'm not likely to get it, she thought.

'It's just that when I told Nerys and Tina about my prize, Nerys was really shirty.'

'Ignore her,' he replied airily. 'You know what she's like with you – anything that makes you look cleverer than Mia or Jemma, and she's on you like a ton of bricks. Like I've told you a dozen times before, she never had kids of her own and when the girls were little and Mum was still modelling, she looked after them a lot. Well, us boys too, of course, but she was always keener on the girly stuff! Mia's always been her favourite, though. She can't bear to think anyone might outshine her.'

Frankie had pulled a face.

'If you get the grades you need for Newcastle – anything better than Mia's A and two Bs – she'll probably accuse the exam board of making a mistake!' Ned laughed. 'Don't let it get to you.'

'But she also said that if I went to the festival, I'd be insulting your dad. Something about me deliberately going against his principles.'

'Now that's downright crazy,' Ned had said. 'We're all going to the festival, yet she makes it sound as if you're the one rebel in the family! It's true that Dad was pretty anti it when it started a few years back – wrote to the papers and all that stuff. And there's no way he'd let them use our fields, or have access over any part of our property because of the conservation issues. But he's not stupid: he knows he can't stop any of us going. I'm going to be there practically twenty-four/seven.'

'You are?'

'Sure – Kids Out There are running a play area and I'm on the team. Anyway, Dad'll be in Mexico and won't know what's going on, will he? Stop worrying! Now I must get over to Alice's.' He'd grinned at Frankie. 'I might not be back for a while.'

'And you reckon he's really keen on this Alice girl?' Lulu asked, offering a stick of chewing gum to Frankie as the bus crawled past the multiplex cinema.

'Do birds fly?' Frankie murmured. 'He's besotted. It's all, "She's so witty, Frankie; oh, Frankie, she's such fun to be with; oh, Frankie, you will be nice to her won't you? She doesn't know anyone down here." What hope do I have?'

Lulu touched her arm. 'Look at it this way,' she said encouragingly, 'you live in the same house, you know him better than anyone and you can wangle it so you do stuff together. Anyway, she won't be here forever. And if you get into Newcastle Uni, you'll virtually be on Ned's doorstep in Durham. How did the driving lesson go, by the way? Yours, not Alice's.'

'Huh,' said Frankie. 'What driving lesson?'

'The car's nearly out of petrol – really sorry. Tomorrow, I promise.'

That was Sunday afternoon.

'Did I say today? Oh sorry, I promised to drive Alice down to Sussex so she can load the horse into the trailer herself. Tomorrow, OK? Absolutely definite.'

That was Monday.

But when Tuesday came, he was cleaning the stable and having a riding lesson with Alice, who stayed for lunch and tea then dragged him off to the cinema. Although 'dragged' was hardly the word to describe the eagerness with which he went.

After the third excuse, Frankie gave up mentioning the subject. Her driving instructor kept reminding her that she needed more practice; she was tempted to ask Mia but she was so preoccupied with scouring rightmove.co.uk for flats in Brighton, uploading pictures of her engagement ring onto Facebook, and telling the world about her forthcoming holiday in Barbados at the Rushworth family villa, that she had no time for anything else. Frankie knew Tina would take her but the last time they had tried it, Tina had screamed 'Stop!' every time their speed reached twenty miles an hour.

First thing on Wednesday morning, Frankie rang the test centre and cancelled her test. It would probably have been too soon anyway.

'Now that,' Lulu declared as the bus pulled into Greyfriars bus station, 'is totally defeatist. Just because Ned's a waste of space . . .'

'No, he's not, he's lovely.'

'*Now* who's besotted?' Lulu teased.

Frankie pulled a face. 'Drop it, OK?' She sighed. 'So – shall we meet for coffee at Leopold's when I'm done at the paper? Eleven-thirty?'

Lulu glanced at her watch. 'Sure,' she replied. 'Then we can hit the shops. I have nothing to wear for the festival.'

An hour later, Frankie was walking down Wellington Street with a broad smile on her face. She'd been interviewed for the following day's edition, and given the prize money, tickets to all three days of M-Brace and a clutch of money-off vouchers for various cafés and clubs in town.

The only thing niggling at the back of her mind was William. When she'd mentioned to the photographer, a ginger-haired guy called Spike, that her brother was a photographer on the *Sea Siren*, he had whistled through his teeth. 'Wow! That is a ticket to serious money if he plays his cards right. He needs to get a few commissions from the blue rinse brigade – make 'em look years younger than they really are – and then brandish his card and hey presto! Before you know it, he'll be getting invites to do the society set all over the world.'

Frankie had laughed knowing that things weren't quite that simple, but it had started her thinking. The last few messages on Facebook from Wills had lacked his usual hilarious, punctuation-free outpourings. They had read more like travelogues, with lots of news about what Malta was like or how he hadn't managed to go ashore at Cagliari because he had to photograph some damage to the swimming pool. In the past he'd been bubbling over with news about his plans, and his Facebook page had been full of new photos for sale; recently he had sounded flat and he hadn't uploaded anything for weeks. Even his last message, congratulating her on her prize, didn't contain one single joke, which for William was a sure sign that things weren't right.

She needed to hear his voice: she would phone him as soon as she got home.

It didn't take Frankie long, while queuing for her latte, to spot Lulu. She was sitting at the rear of Leopold's, the newest café in Northampton, in a red leather chair, legs crossed, skirt hitched up and arms gesticulating wildly at a guy sitting opposite her.

Typical, thought Frankie with amusement, balancing her coffee in one hand and a chocolate-chip muffin in the other and edging her way towards the spare seat next to her friend. Lulu was the kind of girl who struck up conversations with total strangers on trains and buses, particularly if they were male and under twenty-five.

'Hiya!' Lulu waved at her and pulled the chair back at the same moment that the guy stood up and turned round.

A bystander would have been hard-pressed to decide which of them looked the more amazed.

'It's you!' he said to Frankie.

'What are you doing here?' Frankie replied.

'Do you two know each other?' Lulu asked.

'This,' said Frankie, 'is Henry Crawford. I was telling you about him.'

'All good I hope.' Henry smiled.

'All *true*,' murmured Frankie and went to find a paper napkin and compose herself.

'Well, thanks for nothing! You frightened him off,' Lulu moaned when Frankie returned to the table. 'I was just getting somewhere.'

'Lulu! I told you about the way he came on to Mia the very night she got engaged.' She had decided to keep quiet about the way he'd flirted with her too – somehow it was humiliating to admit to being cast aside so easily. 'And now he's chatting *you* up – you didn't even know his name!'

'Oh *puh-leese*! You are so uptight! Honestly, you're like something out of a bygone age.' She leant across and pinched a piece of Frankie's muffin. 'Hey, look!' She pointed to the floor. 'He's left his books behind.'

Frankie bent down and picked up the two paperbacks

and a Rexel sleeve stuffed full of pages of illegible scrawl.

'I don't believe it,' she said. '*Little Dorrit* and *Mansfield Park*.'

'Little who?' Lulu's taste in reading was limited to chick-lit and *Grazia* magazine.

'And they're annotated,' Frankie mused, flicking through the pages. 'I wouldn't have thought he . . . I'll just go and see if I can catch up with him.'

'I'll do it,' said Lulu.

But Frankie was already halfway to the door. She had hardly left the café when she spotted Henry hotfooting it up the hill towards her.

'You found them! Thanks so much,' he panted, taking the books from her. 'I don't know what I would have done if I'd lost these. I haven't got round to transferring my latest notes to my laptop yet, lazy sod that I am.'

'So, you're actually reading these?'

'Don't sound so surprised!' He laughed. 'It's part of my course. I'm doing film and theatre design at Ruskin and my summer assignment is to design two sets – a film set for *Dorrit* and a stage set for the Jane Austen. Trouble is, I can't seem to break away from stereotypes – you know, all rats and clanking chains or lace bonnets and fans!'

'Mmmm,' Frankie said. 'Trouble with Austen is that she's been done to death. Great movies and all that, but most of them are clichéd and half of them nothing like the original.' She screwed up her face. 'You know what? I'd forget all that and focus on the starkness of Dorrit's life experience and the shallowness of the society of Austen's time. In fact, you could do a modern . . .' She stopped short, furious that she could be so influenced by his choice of reading material.

'A modern . . .?'

'Nothing, I must go. Lulu will be getting in a strop,' she said hastily.

'And I'm due at the Royal Theatre,' he said, glancing at his watch. 'My father wangled a meeting with the stage manager and I daren't be late. There's a chance I might be able to shadow her for a week later in the summer.'

'That would be so cool,' Frankie enthused, despite herself. 'They're doing Ibsen next month. Good luck!'

'See you around,' Henry said. 'I want to hear your ideas!'

'Sure,' Frankie replied and then mentally kicked herself for sounding so enthusiastic. *He may be more interesting than you thought*, she told herself firmly, *but remember he can't be trusted.*

'I'll come over sometime and we can talk theatre,' he called after her.

She knew that was probably just an excuse to see Mia again, but to her great annoyance the idea of talking to him suddenly seemed rather more attractive than she would have imagined.

CHAPTER 6

'Selfishness must always be forgiven,
you know, because there is no hope for a cure.'
(Jane Austen, *Mansfield Park*)

A WEEK LATER, FRANKIE WAS SITTING ON THE SWING SEAT in the garden, eyes half closed, attempting to resolve an impossible situation in her story about the character called Jasper. She was trying to write to distract herself from worrying about her mother. She'd just come back from a fleeting visit to Hove, where the doctor had suggested her mother would soon be ready to leave for another try at a halfway house placement – which of course was good in one way, but worrying too, because it might not work out. Suddenly she heard her name being called.

'Frankie! Oh, thank goodness I've found someone!' It was Alice, trim in a pair of cream jodhpurs and an open-neck shirt, struggling with a saddle over one arm and a bridle, rope halter and hay net over the other. Since her horse had arrived, she'd been visiting the house twice a day and somehow managing to hang about for far longer than Frankie thought was necessary. 'Where's Ned?'

'He's helping Nerys move her stuff,' Frankie replied stiffly. 'Her boiler finally gave up the ghost and apparently the dogs get traumatised by workmen so she's moving into the house.'

'I would have thought that any animal who could cope with your aunt Nerys would find a couple of gas fitters a doddle,' she said.

Frankie struggled to suppress her laughter and failed. She had to admit that, like her brother, Alice could be very witty, and if she hadn't been after Ned, Frankie might well have regarded her as a friend.

'Sorry, that wasn't very kind, was it?' Alice admitted. 'So I guess she'll keep Ned occupied for ages?'

'Probably. Tina's gone away to a health spa with an old school friend so Nerys is in charge. And don't we all know it!'

'I bet.' Alice laughed. 'So . . . I don't suppose – well, would you . . . Could you possibly . . .?'

'What?'

'Help me with these?' She hitched the saddle higher up her arm and brandished the halter. 'And do the gates while I try to catch Fling and get him into the stable? He's been somewhat spooked by the move and I want to get him indoors before they start testing the sound systems again for the festival. That high-pitched whistle freaks him out.' She looked pleadingly at Frankie. 'I don't reckon I can manage everything on my own.'

'OK, as long as I don't have to go near the horse,' Frankie replied. 'They scare me rigid.'

She waited for some sarcastic reply but Alice simply nodded. 'With me, it's caterpillars,' she said.

'Caterpillars?'

'Mmm, the way they loop along and their bodies are all squidgy and furry and – yuck!'

She shivered and handed the halter and bridle to Frankie as they began to walk across the lawn and round the back of the house.

'What's going on in there?' She gestured through the conservatory window, where a man and a woman were setting up reflectors and umbrellas and fiddling with a camera on a tripod.

'*Country Life*,' Frankie told her. 'They're about to take the engagement photograph of Mia and Nick.'

Alice pulled a face. 'Very upmarket,' she said. 'Don't you find it hard?'

'Hard? What do you mean?'

'Well, fitting in here,' Alice said. 'Poppy told me that you'd had a pretty dire childhood and you weren't exactly wealthy.'

'Oh, that makes me somehow inferior does it?' Frankie blurted out. 'That and not being a *live wire*!'

The moment the words were out of her mouth she regretted them. She wasn't proud of eavesdropping and, despite her feelings, she hated to embarrass anyone deliberately.

'Live wire? What do you mean,' Alice cried, clearly

having missed the allusion. 'I do this all the time – I open my mouth before engaging my brain. I wasn't saying you were inferior, honestly. I'm so sorry. What I meant was, you're more like me and Henry than the Bertrams.'

'Hardly,' Frankie said. 'For one thing, I didn't go to a posh boarding school.'

'Our school wasn't posh and we only went because my mother couldn't wait to get us out of the way so that she could devote herself to a succession of different men,' Alice said bitterly. 'And you know what? Even now, all these years on, I feel so angry at what she did. I mean – how could she?' She kicked at the gravel on the pathway to the paddock. 'She woke us up in the middle of the night – we were only eight at the time – and dragged us off to Cornwall to this man Derek. She left a note for my father: *Can't do this any more*, it said. Can you believe that?'

Frankie bit her lip. 'My dad . . .' she began and then thought better of it. Family loyalty, she thought, counted for something.

'See?' Alice replied. 'I knew you'd understand – that's why I felt a connection the moment I met you. Henry feels the same, I guess; he's been seeing quite a bit of you, hasn't he? Didn't he come over yesterday when you got back from Hove?' Her eyes twinkled as she winked at Frankie.

'What? Oh, no it's nothing like *that*,' she said hastily. 'He just came over to talk about his project.'

'Hey! It's no problem. He likes you, he told me so.

What's more, I happen to know he told one of his mates that you were cute and have got a lot of untapped potential. Which for Henry is as good as saying he's smitten.'

Frankie smiled and shrugged, unsure of her feelings about this latest revelation. 'So did you live in Cornwall for a long time?' she said, desperate to change the subject.

'You're blushing,' Alice teased. 'I'll tell Henry he's in with a good chance!'

'No, don't! I . . .'

'Just teasing,' she laughed. 'And in answer to your question, Mummy got tired of Derek a couple of years later and moved us on to Liverpool – that was Aidan – and now she's with Greg in East Grinstead. He's a real slimeball, which is why we're here with Dad and —'

'Yes, that's it. That's absolutely it!' Frankie stopped short when she realised she was speaking out loud.

'*What's* it?'

She could hardly tell Alice that the saga of her mother's erratic love life had just triggered a brilliant twist to the Jasper story that had been taxing her.

'Nothing – I mean, I knew that was why you were here.'

They had reached the paddock and Alice took the halter from Frankie's hand. 'Come on, Fling,' she called. 'We need to get you ready for Ned's lesson.' She turned to Frankie. 'He's a cutie, isn't he? A real sweetheart.'

'I guess.' Frankie shrugged. 'Like I said, I don't know anything about horses.'

'Not Fling, silly! Ned. Although I suppose seeing as

how you are cousins, you don't see it. But believe me, he's one fit guy. And you know what?

'What?'

'I'm pretty sure he likes me. I'm useless at this driving lark – my last instructor gave up on me in the end and Dad finds reasons to put off taking me out, even though he shelled out loads to get me insured on his car – but Ned's so patient, and I'm sure that's because he fancies me. By the way, your test was last week, wasn't it? I'm sure Ned said. How did you get on?

'I cancelled it.'

'What on earth for?'

'I need loads more practice.' Frankie sighed.

'So get Ned to take you out,' Alice said airily. 'Like I said, he's really patient.'

'And always round your place,' Frankie muttered, and then immediately regretted it.

'Oh, I get it! I'm sorry – I didn't realise. Well, don't worry, I'll tell him to take you too,' Alice declared. 'He said he'd do anything I asked – isn't that sweet? I'll sort it, OK?'

'No, I . . .'

'Enough!' Alice said. 'I've messed up again because I'm a self-centred cow wanting him all to myself and now I'm going to put it right. Am I forgiven?'

'Of course,' Frankie murmured. What else could she say?

'That's good.' Alice grinned. 'Because, to be honest, I guess I'll never change! Come on, open the gate, will you?'

* * *

Frankie was on her way back to the house, eager to get her latest idea onto her laptop, when her thoughts were rudely interrupted by a motorbike roaring its way up the drive, throwing up gravel and screeching to a halt at the front door. Its rider, clad from head to toe in leathers despite the warmth of the day, leapt off the bike and, taking the steps to the entrance in a single stride, pulled off his helmet.

Frankie did a double take. The guy was black with close-cropped hair and a pair of diamond nose studs. As she drew near he turned, and ran down the steps towards her.

'Well hi! Now let me guess. You're Jemma? No? Mia then.'

Frankie shook her head. 'Frankie,' she said.

'Aha – the cousin rescued from the pits of poverty.' He nodded. 'I've heard about you.'

Frankie bit her lip so hard she could taste blood on her tongue. 'Are you looking for someone?' she asked curtly.

'James. Where is he?'

'Mexico,' Frankie replied.

'That's where you're wrong,' he said, glancing at a flashy watch on his wrist. 'See, he sent me a text not three hours ago to say he'd landed at Heathrow and needed to see me, like now. Sounded really hassled.'

'But he's not due back for another week,' Frankie said.

'That's what I thought,' he said. 'Jump Leads – that's our band – lost the festival slot because of James going off all of a sudden. Then Skid – he's our keyboard player

– blew a fuse and has gone off backpacking with some mates, and Natalie – she does backing vocals – has jacked us in for good.' He kicked at the gravel. 'It's a total mess.' He sighed. 'I'm Jon, by the way. Jon Yates.'

'Oh yes, James has talked about you. You're a rapper, right?' Despite their bad start, Frankie couldn't help liking this guy.

He grinned. 'Rapper, songwriter, street dancer – you name it, I'm it!' he said. 'In between I write freelance stuff on the music scene for whichever paper will take it! Even the *Daily Telegraph* – get that! Mind you, my godfather works there which helps. So, are you going to ask me in or what?'

To her great relief, Frankie caught sight of Nerys staggering up the driveway from Keeper's Cottage, her face almost completely masked by the enormous dog basket she was carrying. She was about to call out to her when Nerys dumped the basket down and waved officiously in their direction.

'Young man! YOUNG MAN!'

Jon looked at her in surprise.

'And about time too,' Nerys stormed, striding over to him. 'You call this premier service? Twelve pounds a month I pay British Gas for the privilege of hanging about all morning waiting for you to show up. It's simply not good enough and I've a mind to write —'

'Nerys, this is Jon Yates. He's nothing to do with British Gas. He's a friend of James,' Frankie explained hastily.

'What? You're Jon? But you're . . . really? How very

strange.' She eyed Jon up and down suspiciously. 'Well, he's out of the country so you've had a wasted journey.' She sniffed.

Frankie was about to explain the situation when Ned appeared round the side of the house.

'Is that the lot, Nerys? You're only going to be here for a few days and there's enough stuff to — Oh, sorry! I didn't realise . . .'

'This young man says he's a friend of James,' Nerys announced, in a tone of voice that suggested that she would prefer to believe that Thornton Parslow had been taken over by aliens.

'Jon!' A look of recognition crossed Ned's face. 'Hi, how are you doing? Remember me? Ned, James's brother? We met at that gig in London.'

'Oh sure, I remember – you're Golden Boy.'

'I wish people would stop . . .' Ned retorted, colour flooding his face.

'Hey, lighten up, man!' Jon laughed. 'I'm just joking.'

Ned shrugged. 'Anyway, James is away, I'm afraid.'

'So who's that then?' Jon said as a black cab drove up to the house and a holdall was flung from the door, followed by a dishevelled-looking James. 'Hey, mate, good to see ya!'

Jon threw an arm round James's shoulder as he climbed out of the taxi and slapped him on the back.

'James? What are you doing back so soon? Where's Dad?' Ned asked. 'Is something wrong?'

'Wrong? Depends how you look at it,' James said.

'Where is Dad?' Ned asked again.

'Still shouting the odds in Mexico, I guess. Not that I give a damn.'

The expression on his face suggested to Frankie that his last remark was a total lie.

'But how come he agreed to let you come back?' Ned persisted.

'I said it was wrong to let the band down,' James mumbled. 'Besides, he was quite happy to be rid of me.'

'Really? But I thought Dad wanted you to —'

'Dad wanted, Dad wanted – well, for once, Dad's not getting his own way. And if you knew the things he's . . . Oh, forget it! Now be a good little brother and pay the cab, will you? I'm skint.'

With that, he picked up his bag and, with Jon hard on his heels, disappeared into the house.

Friend Request.

Henry Crawford has invited you to be a friend on Facebook. Accept/ignore.

Frankie hesitated. She couldn't very well press *ignore* – he'd be sure to want an explanation. She pressed *accept* – after all, she didn't have to take any notice of his posts; she could say she rarely went online. The moment she pressed *accept*, his profile came up and there he was, smiling confidently. Under *About me* he had written, *I'm young, fit, open to all sorts of offers, as long as they involve fun and pushing the boundaries. Check me out, babes!*

'Typical!' she muttered, her eyes scanning the extensive list of his friends. She had to admit his profile threw up some interesting and unexpected facts about him

– the plays he'd seen, his love of Chekhov, Alan Ayckbourn and Harold Pinter, and his ambition to work in theatres on every continent of the world. She was about to write him a message (Pinter she simply didn't get), when a message popped up at the corner of her screen.

Hi Frankie!
Sorry I couldn't chat for long when you phoned last week but as I said, the big boss was floored with a sickness bug and I had to do the photos for the Fancy Dress Ball. Then I caught the bug and thought I was going to die.

Frankie smiled to herself. William had many attributes but putting up with illness wasn't one of them.

Thrilled about your prize. I'd heard about Thomas's award before you told me – I read the papers online and his photo caught my eye. Well done him. Well, time to come clean: the other reason I have been slow getting back to you is because I have been putting off bad news. Siren Lines are going out of business; it's been on the cards for some time, with passenger numbers dropping and the state of the two ships pretty inadequate by today's standards. So I've got to find another job. Any ideas? Got to go – spotted dolphins and want to get some shots to add to my website. Sold two prints of Mount Etna last week so at least there's that to fall back on. More later xxx :)

Frankie was overcome by a surge of guilt. She had it so easy – and there was William, only three years older, having to earn every penny for himself with just the small allowance that Thomas gave him to top up his meagre salary. That's why she saw so little of him – every time he was on leave from the ship, he would dash up to Northamptonshire, spend a couple of days with her, and then go to Hove to visit their mum and earn money at whatever fast-food chain or pier café took him on.

She typed back.

Really sorry about the job – but you're so good I'm sure you'll find something soon. What do you most want to do? Mia and Nick have spent all morning being photographed by Country Life *– I bet you could do that with your hands tied behind your back. Not that you'd want to – it's all so pretentious. Could you get a job with a newspaper? The guy who took my picture was*

The sound of a car crunching to a halt below had her dashing to the window. Alice had promised to make Ned take Frankie out as soon as she had finished her turn and she watched as the bright yellow Peugeot crunched to a halt. The driver's door flew open and she saw Alice, head tipped back, roaring with laughter. Frankie's gaze took in her long, tanned legs, the minuscule white shorts and the high-heeled strappy sandals, totally unsuitable for a driving lesson.

Alice swung her legs out of the car and in an instant,

the passenger door opened and he was there, taking her hand as she tossed the car keys at him. Deftly he caught them, pocketed them – and still held onto her hand. They seemed to be in freeze frame: neither of them moving, they stood staring into one another's eyes.

Frankie held her breath. She wanted to turn away, pretend that none of this was happening, but she couldn't move. Slowly he raised a hand, and gently brushed a tendril of hair from Alice's face. His hand slid down her cheek as he pulled her towards him.

Frankie swallowed, her heart thumping in her chest. *Don't do it. Please, don't do it. Not her. Not now.*

Their lips met. Watching, Frankie could almost feel the tenderness of the kiss, the shiver down the spine as hands caressed one another. And then the car, the figures and the surrounding garden became a blur as the tears spilled down her cheeks.

She was a fool, an idiot, a complete fantasist. What made her think for even one second that she stood a chance with Ned? Even before Alice appeared on the scene, she'd just been little cousin Frankie and the only reason he'd taken any notice of her at all was because he was a kind and thoughtful person. Come to think of it, he probably saw her in the same light as one of his youth projects – let's help poor Frankie who comes from a broken home.

Well, sod him. Sod Alice. Sod all of them.

She was wiping mascara off her cheeks fifteen minutes later when she heard footsteps running up the stairs. The door opened and Alice, flushed and breathing heavily, burst in.

'Knock, why don't you?' Frankie muttered.

'Sorry,' Alice panted. 'I'm all over the place.'

All over Ned, more like, Frankie thought bitterly.

'Ned's in the kitchen waiting for you,' Alice went on. 'I've got to go and see to Fling, but I so need to talk to you when you get back. Something amazing's happened and I've just got to tell someone! Hey, are you OK?'

'Fine.'

'You've been crying.' Alice took a step closer to her. 'Can I help?'

You can back off, thought Frankie. *You can go back to East Grinstead on a one way ticket*.

'No, I'm fine, really,' she muttered. 'Must dash. Can't keep Ned waiting.'

And with that she pushed past Alice and ran downstairs and into the kitchen, expecting to find Ned on his own. Instead, she found half the family there: James, gazing miserably into a mug of coffee, was slumped at the table next to Jemma and Jon, while Mia perched on the granite worktop and Ned, a frown creasing his forehead and a can of Pepsi in one hand, leant against the larder fridge.

'I just can't believe that you cancelled our slot at M-Brace for nothing!' Jon was storming. 'You're here now – we could have gone ahead. In fact, why did you bother coming back for the festival if —'

'What did you say?' Suddenly James was alert and staring at his friend.

'I said, why did you cancel —?'

'Are you telling me *you* didn't cancel the slot?' James said.

'Course not! You said you'd do it when you phoned me from the airport, remember? Said you'd do it right away.' Jon's eyes widened. 'Are you telling me you forgot?'

James nodded, a grin spreading across his face. 'I did,' he said. 'Which means we're still on. We're in business!'

Frankie stared at him, her forehead puckering in a frown. She remembered him saying that he'd come back from Mexico because he couldn't let the band down – but if he assumed they weren't playing anyway . . . then what was the *real* reason he'd rushed back so unexpectedly?

'We are in business!' James repeated and for a moment Jon looked as excited as his friend, but then his face clouded.

'No we're not.' He sighed. 'When you left, Skid and Nat went off in a huff and without them . . .' He paused. 'Unless . . .'

'Unless what?' James said.

'I'm the front man, right? My lyrics, my rapping, my stand-up routine? This whole thing is about showcasing my stuff.'

'And the band's,' James said.

'And I'm here,' John went on. 'You're the drummer and you're here. So if we could just rework —'

'Come off it,' James protested. 'We've only got till the weekend and without Skid on the keyboard and Nat's vocals —'

'Like I said, we rework it,' Jon interrupted. 'Listen, I need to get my routine noticed and let's face it, the rest of you have always been just back up.'

'Well, thanks!'

'You know what I mean,' Jon said impatiently. 'So . . . it's new talent night, right? Let's get some new talent! What about you lot?' He gestured round the room. 'We need a vocalist and a keyboard player. And if we could get the girls to do a dance routine to fill the slot left by Nat's solo . . .'

'That is just the coolest idea!' Mia cried.

'Do you really think it could work?' Jemma asked.

'Anything that means I can get on that stage is worth trying,' Jon said decisively. 'I'd given up all hope without James – but now he's back . . .' He paused. 'But we do need a girl who can —'

'Who needs a girl?'

Alice peered round the door, giving a little four-fingered wave to Ned who, to Frankie's disgust, adopted the facial expression of a salivating puppy.

'This is Alice,' he said, turning to his brother. 'I told you about her.'

'Charles Grant's daughter, I know.' James gestured to an empty chair and grinned at her. 'Hi! Can you dance?'

Alice frowned. 'Like, can birds fly? I did tap, disco, modern, the lot when I was a kid. I was pretty good, won cups and everything.'

I bet you were, Frankie thought. *If there was an A-level in self-esteem you'd get an A-star.*

'Why do you want to know?' Alice asked.

'Don't ask,' Ned muttered.

'Ignore my brother,' James said. 'He sees having fun as one of the seven deadly sins.'

Alice shot a quizzical look at Ned. 'In which case,' she said, smiling at him, 'he needs someone to show him a good time. So what's all this about anyway?'

'M-Brace,' James said. 'Jon here has cooked up this great act. Usual band stuff, backing vocals and all that, but then he does some stand-up and rap.'

'And a bit of street dancing thrown in,' said Jon. 'The basics are all there but we need to do some improvising fast. So come on, who's up for it?'

'Me!' Mia's hand shot up.

'You bet,' Jemma added hastily.

'Bring it on,' Alice said, wiggling her hips and waving her hands in the air.

'Only one problem.' Jon sighed. 'We still haven't worked out how to get a guitarist.'

'No problem,' James declared. 'Ned's a pretty good guitar player. Grade eight and all that!'

'Hang on, there's no way you're roping me in,' Ned said firmly. 'I'm going to be tied up.'

'What you mean, *tied up*? It's the holidays, for God's sake,' James said. 'Don't tell me you're like Dad – all festivals are Bad Things.'

'Might disturb a few stag beetles and the odd otter,' Mia chipped in sarcastically.

'As it happens, I'll be tied up *at* the festival,' Ned replied. 'KOT's doing this massive promotion.'

'Cots? You're selling cots at a rock fest?' Alice asked.

'No,' Ned laughed. 'KOT – it stands for Kids Out There. I do placements with them whenever I'm not at uni – working with disadvantaged kids from inner cities and giving them adventure holidays. The festival organisers wanted an area for kids to play and we decided to run it. It'll be great publicity for the charity and the money parents pay will fund holidays for the kids. There's a whole team of us manning a climbing wall and zip wire and stuff.'

'Wow, Ned, that's amazing!' To Frankie's surprise James sounded really interested. 'Is it just kids locally?'

'No, nationwide,' Ned said, clearly pleased that his brother was showing an interest. 'It started —'

'Never mind all that,' Alice broke in. 'Fact is, if there's a whole team, they can do without you, can't they? Cancel – this'll be far more of a laugh.'

'And we need you,' James said.

'For the last time, no,' Ned said. 'End of.'

'You know what, Ned?' Alice challenged, tossing her head. 'Poppy said you were boring and I didn't believe her. But I'm beginning to think she was right.'

For a moment, Ned said nothing. Then he tossed his empty drinks can into the bin and walked to the door. Alice deftly stepped in front of him, blocking his way. 'Come on, prove me wrong,' she said, tipping his chin with her finger. 'Do it for me. Remember, only an hour ago you said you'd do anything to make me happy.'

Frankie's stomach lurched into her mouth and her throat went dry. Ned's face turned a livid shade of red.

'Oooh, get you!' Jemma teased. 'Ned's in *lurve*!'

'And this would make me very happy,' Alice said. 'Please, pretty please.'

'Come on, Ned,' James said. 'You can't get all precious about it because, actually, it's right up your street. Jon's rapping is all about social justice and all that kinda stuff. I thought that's what you were about?'

'I am, but —'

'Sorted!' Alice cried, clapping her hands and planting a kiss on his cheek.

'Alice, I can't. KOT needs me, and anyway, gigs aren't my thing,' Ned replied.

'Well, in that case, maybe I'm not your thing either,' Alice muttered, her face like thunder. 'Cause if there's anything worse than a guy who's boring, it's one who doesn't mean what he says.'

Ned stared at her for a moment and then turned away. 'Frankie, are you coming?' he said, not meeting her gaze. 'I've only got half an hour so if you want to drive . . .'

'I'm ready.' She moved to the door, which was still blocked by a now slightly petulant-looking Alice.

'You'll make him see sense, won't you, Frankie?' she pleaded. 'This sounds like such an great idea – we can't let him ruin it.'

'So leave Ned alone and get your brother to join in instead,' Frankie replied tartly. 'I'm sure he'd love it. He's into all that stage stuff.'

'No use if he doesn't play anything,' James muttered sulkily.

'But he does,' Alice replied. 'Sax pretty badly and keyboard really well.'

'Well, why didn't you say?' Jon cried. 'Where is he? Get him here right now!'

'Frankie, that's an amazing idea!' Mia burst out. 'Alice, text him – he'd be so up for it. And hey, Charlie Maddox plays guitar, right? So we're sorted!' She turned to Ned. 'Henry and Charlie know how to have fun – you should take lessons.'

Too late, Frankie realised what she had done. After what she'd seen at the party, Mia and Henry were probably best kept apart. 'Surely Nick'll want to get involved?' she suggested hastily.

'Nick? He doesn't play anything. And have you heard him sing? Sounds like a cat in deep distress!' Mia giggled. 'But you're right – when he hears about this, he's sure to want to be in on it. And he'll sulk if there's nothing for him to do.'

'I do need a stooge, a kind of fall guy for the stand-up routine,' Jon said. 'Someone who doesn't mind standing there, being the butt of the jokes and looking an idiot.'

'Perfect.' Mia nodded. 'That is so totally Nick.'

That's not exactly the remark of an adoring fiancée, Frankie thought as she followed Ned through the hall and out onto the drive.

'You don't think she meant it, do you? About me not being her thing? Frankie, are you listening?'

'I'm trying to get across this roundabout,' Frankie replied through clenched teeth.

'Sorry. You're doing really well. Only I can't back out of helping with the charity promotion now, and even if I could, I'm not into all this street dance, rapping stuff. Do you think I'm being a bore? I don't want her to hate me but —'

'NED!' Frankie yelled. 'Will you just shut up for a minute while I try to concentrate?'

'Sorry,' Ned mumbled. 'Hey, you're in the wrong lane.'

'Oh, what a surprise,' she retorted. 'Like, nothing was distracting me, was it?'

'Sorry.'

'Stop saying sorry!' she snapped, flipping the indicator on and edging into the inside lane. 'Can we go somewhere quieter? I need to practise parallel parking.'

They drove in silence for a few minutes. 'I just don't know what to do,' Ned sighed, as Frankie began gingerly reversing into a space between a mud-covered four by four and a gleaming Fiat Punto. 'If I don't join in, Alice'll hate me, and if I do, I'll be letting the KOT team down and I'll hate myself.'

Frankie put her foot on the brake, threw the gear into neutral and turned off the engine. She turned to face Ned. 'If Alice is going to hate you just because you are doing something for someone else, then she's not worth worrying about.'

Ned chewed his lip. 'I know she sounded off, but underneath she's not like that,' he protested. 'You mustn't think badly of her. She's been through some tough times and I'd have thought that you of all people would understand that.' The critical tone in his voice cut her to the core.

'I do, but the work you do with KOT means a lot to you – why can't she see that?'

'That's not fair,' he replied. 'I mean, imagine you're Alice – just for a minute. You have to admit, you'd be trying to persuade me to do the gig, wouldn't you?'

Frankie took a deep breath. 'No,' she said. 'I wouldn't.'

'But if you – well, I mean if you were, kind of, maybe keen on me, then you would?'

The irony of the question made Frankie's cheeks flush and she had to turn to look out of the car window.

'Well?' Ned persisted. 'You would, wouldn't you?'

She turned to face him, making herself meet his gaze.

'Ned.' She sighed. 'What part of the word "No" don't you get?'

'James, wait!'

Ned had just dropped Frankie off at the front of the house and was turning the car round to dash off to help prepare the KOT stand when James and Jon came out of the house and headed for Jon's motorbike.

'Can't stop,' James called back. 'Things to do.'

Ned jumped out of the car and ran over to them as Jon fired up the bike.

'No wait! Look, ever since you got back you've been acting weird; up one minute, down the next and as prickly as hell. So tell me, what really went on in Mexico?' Ned demanded. 'I get the feeling you're hiding something.'

Frankie edged nearer, struggling to catch his words above the noise of the Harley Davidson.

'Dad wanted me to learn stuff out there, right?' she heard James shout, climbing onto the back of the bike. 'Well, I did. I learnt a lot – and that I don't ever want to have anything to do with him or his lousy business, ever!'

'But you're happy to spend the money he makes,' Ned snapped back. 'Happy to have him clear your debts.'

James stared at his brother, his jaw working. 'I was, once upon a time,' he said. 'But not any more. I swear to you, Ned, I don't want a single penny of his money. Ever again. Not now I know what goes into making it.'

And with that, he climbed back onto the bike, slapped Jon on the shoulder and they roared off down the drive.

'Trust James,' Ned muttered to Frankie. 'He sees how hard Dad has to work and decides he can't hack it.'

Frankie stared at him. Was that really what James meant? It didn't seem to be enough of a reason for the vehemence in his words.

'I guess you're right,' she replied. But deep down, she wasn't at all sure.

CHAPTER 7

*'A young woman, pretty, lively . . .
was enough to catch any man's heart.'*
(Jane Austen, *Mansfield Park*)

'I DON'T KNOW WHAT YOU'RE GETTING IN SUCH A TIZZ about,' Lulu remarked the following day, as she and Frankie walked through the village on the way to play tennis. 'So Ned's changed his mind – big deal!'

'She's just twisting him round her little finger,' Frankie replied. 'It makes me sick.'

'Sure it does,' Lulu agreed. 'Sick because you didn't have the courage to make a play for him yourself. Just forget him – you're wasting your time.'

Frankie said nothing, largely because she had a horrible feeling that her friend was right. Earlier that morning, she had bumped into Ned, guitar case slung over his shoulder, heading for the old playroom.

'What's with the guitar?' she had asked abruptly.

'I've decided to do it,' he had replied. 'I mean, it's only fair when you think about it.'

'Do what?' she had demanded, although she had a pretty good idea.

'Play for this band,' he had replied.

'But you said —'

'I know what I said,' he had snapped, 'but Alice made me see I was being a killjoy. The band have worked hard and maybe this is the break James needs – he could certainly do with cheering up.'

He sounded, thought Frankie, as if he was snatching at straws, finding any reason to do what Alice wanted.

'And like Alice says, family should come first.'

Alice says, *Alice says*, Frankie had chanted silently in her head.

'So what about the charity?' she had asked. 'You can't just turn your back on them.'

'I was stupid,' he'd replied. 'Alice made me see that too. The festival's on for three days – there will be plenty of time for me to help out.' He had paused. 'And actually, she came up with a brilliant idea.'

'What?'

'You could cover my Saturday morning slot – well, and Friday teatime come to that. Like Alice says, that will free me up for the final rehearsals and it's not like you'd miss out watching us because we're not on till five in the afternoon.' He had smiled nervously. 'So – will you?'

She had stared at him. *You must think I'm mad*, she'd thought. *Just because you want to spend your time drooling over Alice, you expect me to cover for you. Good old Frankie, she'll do it. She's a soft touch. After all, Frankie hasn't got a life. Well, you can think again, because no way —*

'Will you? Please?' he'd said. 'For me?'

She had taken a deep breath. *It's time*, she told herself, *you stopped being a doormat.*

'Of course I will,' she had said. 'What time do I start?'

Now, heading for the tennis-club pavilion and remembering her total lack of gutsiness, she slammed her tennis racquet against her thigh.

'Idiot!' she said out loud.

'Who are you calling idiot?' Lulu demanded.

'Me,' Frankie said. 'Why am I so feeble? How come I spent ages listening to Alice going on and on at me about how Ned kissed her and how she's never felt like this about any guy ever – and then I go and make things even easier for the two of them?'

Lulu squeezed her hand. 'You're in love,' she said, 'and they say that makes fools of all of us. I should be so lucky as to find out.' She turned to Frankie. 'Speaking of which, I need you to get me together with James, right? Any excuse, I don't care. Just do it.'

Frankie sighed. James had been acting strangely ever since he got back from Mexico. One minute, he and Jon would be playing music at a zillion decibels, the next he would be storming out of the house, saying he needed space and telling everyone to get off his back. And when Jemma had shown him a piece about Thomas in the *Daily Mail*, James had snatched the paper from her hand

and shredded the page, scattering the pieces all over the floor before stomping out of the room.

'So will you?' Lulu persisted.

'I'm not sure it's a good idea,' Frankie replied.

'Of course it is. It's fate that he came back from Mexico – my stars said I would meet a man from overseas who would fall captive to my charms.'

'He's not from overseas,' Frankie giggled. 'He was only away for ten days.'

'Stop splitting hairs,' Lulu said. 'A girl has to hope.'

The rain started on the Friday, just hours before the festival opened. Throughout the previous day, the roads to the three Thorntons had been clogged with traffic and when Frankie, more eager to improve her driving than to avoid Henry, had agreed to let him take her out in Tina's car for a practice, it had taken them twenty minutes to get past the caravans and trailers edging their way along the lanes. Tents had sprung up, guy rope to guy rope, in fields and meadows and on the local playing field and, at the far end of Thornton Lacey, an area had been given over to yurts and tepees for those with a desire for luxury. The hammering and drilling that had been the background noise from dawn to dusk for the past week ceased, to be replaced by the blaring of loudspeakers directing campers, the tinny jangling of ice-cream and burger vans and the high-pitched whistle of sound systems being tested for the final time. *TV East*'s outside broadcast van was parked near the main stage, within sight of the Park House stables, where

Alice's horse spent most of his time kicking at the door and sending Nerys's two dogs into paroxysms of barking.

The band had been rehearsing tirelessly and Frankie had done her best to keep out of the way, largely because she couldn't stomach the sight of Ned strumming on the guitar while Alice gyrated in front of him and Mia danced around the keyboard, wiggling her bum at Henry and giving him what Frankie considered blatant come-ons whenever Nick wasn't looking. Jemma was in a big sulk because it had been clear within ten minutes of the first run-through that she couldn't dance, and when James pointed out that both Alice and Mia had strong voices and she could hardly be heard at all, she threw a strop, stormed out and told them all what they could do with their act.

'You know what?' she had stormed to Frankie. 'I wouldn't be part of their stupid act if they paid me! If Alice wasn't around, they'd be only too pleased to have me but oh no! Just because she's a size six and up herself, everyone's all over her. She wouldn't even be here twenty-four/seven if Ned didn't have the hots for her!'

Frankie had expected her to cool down, especially when Nerys, who to everyone's surprise seemed very excited by the whole idea of the band, told her she was being silly and that a bit of singing and dancing practice would put her right. But Jemma just told her to butt out, and shut herself in the kitchen, where she banged about with mixing bowls, until the smell of freshly baked cakes and what Frankie sincerely hoped was Jemma's amazing caramel shortbread filled the air.

Cooking was to Jemma what writing was to Frankie: the only thing that could make her feel better however bad the day.

With everyone occupied, Frankie had peace and quiet to finish her story, phone her mum (always a lengthy process and something that left her feeling oddly depleted) and catch up on her reading list for uni. Not that she reckoned she'd get into her first choice; when she'd had an offer from Newcastle she'd been over the moon and when Loughborough and Bristol both made the same offers, she felt she had it made. But now she felt differently; she was sure she'd made a total hash of her A2s and would probably end up doing some dead-end job in between retakes.

She was, in short, in a pretty downbeat frame of mind, which is possibly why things happened the way they did on Friday afternoon.

'What are you doing in here?' Nerys demanded, bustling into the conservatory where Frankie was flicking through uni prospectuses. 'And what's all this mess?' She gestured at the pile of papers beside Frankie's laptop.

She picked up a brochure. 'Mmm.' She sniffed. 'You'll probably get up to your eyeballs in debt – the papers say that most students owe twenty thousand pounds or more.' She eyed Frankie closely. 'I trust you're not getting ideas about asking your uncle to bale you out?'

'Of course not, I —'

'He helped James but then James is his son, and you . . . well, you must learn to stand on your own feet once you leave home,' she declared, picking a dead leaf off the bilbergia.

'I won't exactly be leaving home,' Frankie said snappily. 'I'll be back in the holidays just like the others.'

She smiled to herself, remembering how her uncle had teased her about Newcastle being her first choice, saying she'd come home with a Geordie accent.

'And,' she went on, irritated by the sour expression on Nerys's face, 'I'll get holiday jobs to pay my way, unlike them.'

'That's all right then.' Nerys sniffed again. 'As long as you understand. Like I told your brother, there's only so much charity —'

'William? You've spoken to William? When? What . . .?'

'He phoned this morning,' Nerys said irritably, splashing water from a purple can onto an aloe vera plant. 'He wanted to come and stay next week. Of course, I told him it was out of the question.'

'But why? He always comes here whenever he's got leave.'

'Why? Your uncle is out of the country, Tina is with her friend being detoxified or whatever they call it, and I'm in charge. I can't just go opening their house to all and sundry.'

'He's not all and sundry, he's my brother!' Frankie shouted. 'What's more, he's your nephew.'

'No, Frankie, he's not,' Nerys snapped, 'any more than you are my niece. The sooner you get that into your head the better it will be for all concerned. I seem to have made a mistake bringing you here. You take it all for granted. Now clear up this mess – I'm going to walk the dogs.' With that she turned heel and stomped out of the room.

Frankie snatched her phone from the table and called her brother, tears of frustration spilling down her cheeks.

'This is Wills – sorry I can't take your call . . .'

She grabbed her laptop and Facebooked him.

Nerys told me she said no – she's a cow. But don't worry, it's not up to her. I'll tell Ned – he'll sort her – and then we can find a cheap B and B when we visit Mum. I really want to see you. xx

Frankie got up and stood staring out of the window onto the rain-soaked garden, her stomach churning. How dare Nerys speak to her like that? 'Stupid cow!' She thumped her fist against her thigh and brushed tears of frustration from her cheek.

'So this is where you're hiding.'

She wheeled round to find Henry leaning against the doorpost, chewing gum and looking for all the world as if he owned the place.

'What do you want?' she muttered, turning her back to him and hastily rubbing her eyes. 'I'm busy.'

Within a second his hands were on her shoulders, and she could feel his breath against her neck.

'No you're not,' he replied. 'You've been crying.'

'So what's it to you?' she said, shrugging his hands away. 'Just leave me alone, OK? I'm . . . I'm . . .' She swallowed the words down, knowing that if she said anything more she would blub in front of him and no way was she giving him the satisfaction of seeing her like that.

'You're what? Gorgeous? Fascinating? Sexy?'

'Stop making fun of me!' Frankie snapped. 'You think you're so cool.'

'Hey, chill!' he replied gently, raising his voice above the drumming of rain on the conservatory roof. 'I'm only telling the truth. You are gorgeous and you do fascinate me. A lot.' He brushed her cheek with his finger. 'You're beautiful,' he whispered, 'and later, I'll tell you just what you do to me. But right now . . .' His tone changed to one of briskness and efficiency. '. . . you're needed asap,' he said. 'We want a photograph to stick up on the board at M-Brace – get people interested before our slot. Ned's battery is flat but he says you've got a decent camera.'

Frankie nodded, thankful to be able to change the subject. 'My brother gave me his old Nikon.' At the thought of William and her aunt's spiteful interference, her eyes filled with tears again.

'Hey,' Henry said, cupping her face in his hands. 'What is it?'

'Nothing. Oh, just that William – my brother – has lost his job and he wanted to come and stay but Nerys told him he couldn't. And she had no right – interfering old bat!'

'He's the photographer, right?'

She nodded.

'I guess you two must be really close,' Henry said easily. 'I mean, what with the problems you've had to face. I know that's how it worked with Alice and me.'

He does understand, Frankie thought with surprise.

'We are close,' she admitted. 'When Mum got ill . . .' She hesitated.

'It was you two against the world?' Henry ventured.

She nodded. 'And I so want to see him. He'll be back in a few days. But with Uncle Thomas and Tina away, Nerys is on her high horse and shouting the odds and . . .'

'Maybe Nerys is just having a bad day,' he said. 'Although Nerys on a good day can be pretty daunting, can't she?'

Frankie laughed in spite of herself.

'That's better,' Henry said. 'It's not up to her anyway. Just send Tina a text and get her to deal with it. Job done!'

Frankie nodded. 'You're right,' she said. 'I'm being a wimp.'

'Well,' Henry went on, 'I'm here if ever you need to talk to someone with no axe to grind. OK?'

She nodded, wondering whether perhaps she'd been too hasty in forming her initial opinion of him.

'Oh and by the way, if you want driving practice without having to wait for my sister to leave Ned in peace, I'm your man.'

'Thanks,' she murmured. 'That's really kind.'

'Great.' He smiled. 'So let's get that camera and start shooting.'

'So – what do you think?'

Alice and Mia threw a pose as Frankie adjusted the focus on her camera. They were wearing tiny gold shorts, bra tops studded with strategically-placed fake jewels and gold-glitter dancing shoes.

'You look lovely, Mimi-pops,' Nick said, sidling up to her and sliding his hand down her back.

'For the last time, don't call me that!' Mia snapped. 'Come on, Frankie, get on with it!'

Grateful for the chance to hide behind the viewfinder, Frankie clicked away for several minutes. 'And now all of us!' Jon insisted. 'An action video. In position everyone!'

'Wait!' Frankie said. 'I can't remember how to find the switch to go to video . . .'

'Let me see.' In an instant, Henry was behind her, his arms over her shoulder manipulating the dial. 'There!' he said. 'That should do it.'

And equally quickly, he was back in position at the keyboard.

As Frankie, feeling her cheeks burning, pressed *record*, she saw Mia staring hard at her. The look on her face was one of pure spite.

'Right – action!'

Jon snatched up the mic and began rapping as though the audience was already in front of him. James's drumsticks darted like lightning between bass drum and snare, while Henry, foot tapping and swaying, bashed away on the keyboard. Mia and Alice strutted their stuff, Alice clearly the better dancer, even throwing in a couple of cartwheels during which one of her shoes flew off and hit Nick in the face. Even Nick, the so-called stooge, made a play at lightly clumsy dancing and clapping.

The only one who looked awkward and out of place was Ned. At first his eyes never left Alice, but after a couple of minutes, he began to look distinctly uncomfortable and stared at the ground, twice hitting the wrong chord and earning glares from his brother.

'You know, these stills are good,' Jon said afterwards, taking the camera from Frankie and clicking through the shots. 'We'll get them printed and blown up and start sticking them up round the site. Give me the camera and I'll upload them onto my laptop.'

'So are we done?' Alice asked. 'Because the rain's let up and I've got to get changed and saddle Fling. Ned's going to have his first go at cantering, aren't you, babe?'

'I've just got to take Frankie over to meet the guys from KOT,' he said. 'I won't be long.'

'You'd better not be,' Alice said. 'Fling doesn't like to stand around once he's saddled and ready to go . . .' She smiled at him coyly. 'And neither do I.'

'Has Alice said anything to you? About anything?' Frankie asked Poppy later that evening as they walked to the pub to meet up with some of the old gang from school.

'Frankie, she lives with me, worse luck, and yes, occasionally she deigns to speak,' Poppy teased. 'About what precisely?'

'About her and Ned.' Frankie sighed.

'Now I get it!' Poppy laughed. 'You're jealous.'

'Don't be ridiculous, of course I'm not!' Frankie protested. 'Why . . . should I be?'

'Well,' Poppy went on, 'Alice says that Ned is adorable, has the cutest bum she's ever seen, and comes on to her a bit stronger every time they meet. But you really didn't want to hear that, did you?'

'I don't care.' Frankie shrugged. 'Why would I care? I'm just interested, that's all.'

'There's something else,' Poppy added.

'What?'

'Henry says pretty much the same about you.' Poppy grinned.

Like that's any comfort, Frankie thought. *Although he is nicer than I thought. And definitely fit.*

But he's not Ned.

CHAPTER 8

'You are such a fine speaker that I'm afraid you may actually end in convincing yourself.'
(Jane Austen, *Mansfield Park*)

BY SATURDAY AFTERNOON, THE RELENTLESS RAIN HAD rendered the festival site a quagmire. Tents sagged under the weight of water, hawkers selling transparent brollies did a roaring trade and every event in the indoor arena was packed out. The leaflets that Frankie was supposed to be handing out were sodden within moments of leaving the shelter of the KOT gazebo and mud clung to her boots making every step an effort. Health and Safety had closed the zip-wire attraction as well as the climbing wall and a few disconsolate children were making do with trampolines and ball pits in the large marquee. Ned had never got his riding lesson because the pause in the downpour had only lasted for ten minutes, but Frankie could take little comfort from that. When she had returned to the house the previous evening, she had seen Alice and Ned emerging from Fling's stable and it didn't take a genius to work out the meaning of Ned's dishevelled appearance and the straw sticking to Alice's usually immaculate hair. All in all, the weather reflected the way Frankie felt.

Everyone else, however, seemed to be on a high. Even the fact that having the five o'clock slot wasn't exactly prime time, they were all acting as if they were about to headline at O2. When she got back to the house, splattered with mud and longing for a hot shower, the kitchen had been buzzing. Henry, Jon and Ned were packing instruments in their cases, all set to hike them over to the stage; Alice and Mia were spraying glitter on every part of their anatomy that wasn't covered (which was almost all of it) and Nick was wandering around in pink cords and a paisley waistcoat, asking if he looked OK, and being ignored by everyone. Even Nerys, clad in a waxed jacket and trilby of uncertain age, was filling a Thermos flask and declaring that she was determined to brave what she called 'the screaming masses' to see her beloved niece perform. But the biggest surprise of all was to see Tina perched at the kitchen table, watching the rehearsal video on Jon's laptop and clicking her impeccably manicured fingers in time to the beat.

'Hi Tina, I didn't think you were coming back till Sunday,' Frankie said.

'I wasn't, darling,' Tina replied, 'but to be honest, there's only so much raw food and wheatgrass a woman can stand. And of course, one doesn't like to be away from home for too long – it doesn't do to let other people take over, does it?' She cast a sidelong glance at Nerys and then smiled at Frankie. 'And then there's William to prepare for, isn't there? I'm thrilled he's going to join us.'

Frankie ran over and gave her a hug. 'Thank you,' she said. 'Thank you so much.'

Tina winked at her as Nerys slammed the Thermos flask onto the counter top with unnecessary force.

'I'm so looking forward to seeing him,' she said. 'We all are.'

'Seeing who?' The kitchen door swung open and James, carrying a music stand, eyed his mother sharply. 'Are you telling me Dad's on his way back?'

Frankie glanced at him and was astonished to see a mixture of anger and fear in his eyes.

'I wish,' said Tina with a sigh. 'No darling, we're talking about William – he's coming up for a few days.'

'Great,' James said. 'That's great. Now can we get a move on everyone, please?'

The stage designated for ENT night was on the very edge of the site at the top of the Maddoxes' field, within sight of Park House and hard up against their boundary hedge. To one side was a small tent, in which performers could wait for their slot and tune their instruments. Frankie had arranged to meet up with Lulu, who had spent the whole day drooling over a variety of acts on the main stage. She was waiting for her under a dripping beech tree when Mia, a bright yellow waterproof hiding her skimpy costume, shouted to her from the doorway of the tent.

'Hey, Frankie, over here! Jon wants you.'

Reluctantly Frankie splashed her way through the puddles and into the tent where the band were getting ready.

'I've brought your camera back,' Jon said. 'And I need a favour. Will you take some more photos?'

She nodded.

'Great. So what I want is candid camera – lots of shots. Now, while we're getting set up, and then during the act. And not just us, but close ups of people's expressions while they watch us, mood shots, all that kind of stuff. I want to use them for a collage on the website we're revamping.'

'Actually, I'm waiting for Lulu,' Frankie ventured, swallowing her fury at being spoken to like some kind of hired servant.

'So you can't press a shutter button while talking to a mate?' James said, swigging a can of Red Bull. 'For God's sake, Frankie, it's not like you're contributing in any other way.'

She glanced at Ned for support but he was too busy helping Alice adjust the strap on her top.

'I'm sorry,' James said at once. 'I'm just stressed out and nervous.'

'Relax, man,' Jon said, slapping him on the back. 'You'll be fine. Pretend it's just like any other gig.'

'Sure.' James smiled. 'No sweat. So you'll do the photos, Frankie, yeah?'

'OK,' she agreed. At least Lulu would be happy; she might even manage to get her into a shot with James. 'I'll do what I can.'

As she walked back out into the rain, she couldn't help wondering just what it really was that was stressing James out. Because she was pretty certain that it wasn't anything to do with the band.

'Hey!' James shouted after her, as she walked away. 'You're supposed to be taking pictures of us.'

'You want random reportage,' Frankie retorted. 'That's what you're getting. I'll take you when you're not expecting it.'

'She has a point,' Jon said. 'OK, everyone, final tuning! We've only got twenty minutes to go.'

'Hey, look at that one – isn't he just to die for?'

Lulu peered over Frankie's shoulder as she scrolled through the twenty photos she had taken so far through a gap in the back of the tent as the band got ready – Jon play-punching Nick and yelling at him to stay deadpan; Ned frowning in concentration as he tuned his guitar; Henry yawning and looking bored, a bottle of water in one hand; Alice adjusting her false eyelashes (Frankie hadn't been able to resist catching her when she was pulling a very unflattering face in the mirror) and – the shot that had reduced Lulu to a weak-kneed wreck – James gelling his hair and flexing his shoulders while smiling that slow, languid smile that even Frankie had to admit had a film-star quality about it.

'And you're sure there's no one on the scene,' Lulu

asked, raising her voice above the applause for the act leaving the stage.

Frankie shrugged. 'No one that he's letting on about anyway,' she replied, suddenly wondering if he was acting so uncharacteristically because of girlfriend trouble. 'Hey, look, they're going on stage now. I guess I'd better get closer and start snapping.'

The rain had lessened to a slow drizzle and a glimmer of sunlight was peeking through the mounds of grey clouds, casting light on wet umbrellas. Encouraged by the improvement in the weather, more people were drifting towards the stage as, to a ripple of applause, the band struck up the first number.

Jon was good, Frankie couldn't deny that. His rapping was a sort of gangsta rap but with a political theme – the lyrics were about justice and the underdog, prejudice and tyranny and exploitation, but it was his street dancing that had the crowd on their feet, clapping and cheering at his locking, krumping and popping, the way his body flowed from one move to another without pause. It was clear that he was the star: James was a cool and highly professional drummer and Henry's keyboard playing was great – he really did manage to surprise her – but the girls were merely eye candy and Ned, well, Frankie felt embarrassed for him, he seemed so out of place. As the act progressed, Frankie noticed a camera crew from *East Today* had paused and were training their lens on the stage.

'The black guy – he's good,' she heard one of the men remark. 'Stick with this one for a bit, Carl.'

When Jon started his comedy routine, Frankie focused her lens on Nick. Her heart went out to him – he was trying so hard to respond to Jon's set-up lines, but his eyes kept going to Mia who at that point was leaning provocatively against the keyboard, giving Henry sidelong glances and letting her fingers run across his back. It was, of course, all part of the act but somehow it seemed to Frankie that Mia enjoyed Nick's obvious discomfort and jealousy.

As the band launched into their final number, the heavens opened again. Rain poured down and a flash of lightning lit up the surrounding area. Frankie followed the TV crew's example and edged closer to the stage where the overhang from the roof offered at least a little protection for her lens. She switched the setting so that she could take a succession of shots one after the other and capture the action.

It was a good thing she had, she thought two minutes later; she was so stunned by what she saw that she was sure she would have been unable to press the shutter button. At the end of the song, Mia and Alice turned round, their backs to the audience, whipped off their bra tops, did a quick twirl, blew kisses to the crowd and ran from the stage, as Jon belted out the last line of his song, '*Strip them bare and make them pay!*' The crowd erupted, lewd remarks and wolf whistles filling the air.

'More! More!' someone shouted but a festival organiser stepped speedily onto the stage.

'Fifteen minutes and no encores!' he reminded the crowd and began to introduce the next act.

'I think,' Frankie heard the TV cameraman say, 'that we have that one in the can. The boss said he wanted some local colour and, boy, that's what he's got!'

Later Frankie wished she had thought more about what he was saying, but at the time she had more pressing things to think about.

'Come on, back to the tent,' Lulu ordered. 'This is where you do your best friend bit. Introduce me to James and I'll do the rest.'

She pulled a bottle from her shoulder bag and waved it in Frankie's face. 'Party time!' She giggled. 'And between you and me, it's not water in here! Full strength voddie – and a bit more.'

'LULU! You're not supposed to bring alcohol onto the site.'

Lulu grinned, stuffing the bottle back in her bag. 'I'll just have to make sure me and James get off the site quickly, won't I? Come on, what are we waiting for?

Back in the warm-up tent, Frankie, despite all her efforts, felt totally out of place. Alice and Lulu, high on whatever cocktail Lulu had produced, were flirting outrageously – Alice with Ned and Lulu with James. Mia held hands with Nick and occasionally gave him a kiss, but her eyes constantly followed Henry and it was clear to anyone with half a brain that they were communicating with each other, if not verbally, then through body language and intimate gestures.

When Jemma had turned up ten minutes after the act ended, Frankie had hoped she might slink off with her and watch Apparition, the headline act for the evening, but even Jemma had her own agenda.

'Is that what I think it is?' Jon had cried, as Jemma prised the lid off a huge Cath Kidston cake tin and wafted it under his nose.

'Pineapple cherry cake,' Jemma declared proudly. 'You said you grew up in St Kitts and . . .'

'Oh man!' Jon gasped as Jemma cut the cake into slices. 'I haven't had this since I went to see my gran five years ago. You're amazing!'

Jemma flushed and looked at him coyly. 'Well, hang around and I'll cook you rikkita beef,' she laughed.

'You know how to do that?' Jon spluttered his mouth full of cake. 'How come?'

Jemma shrugged. 'I may be a lousy singer and a pretty useless dancer, but I can pretty much cook anything. Try me!'

Jon grinned. 'Is that an invitation?'

'Uh huh.'

'Great!' he said, dropping his voice. 'Bring it on!'

Witnessing this hot-bed of flirtation and fun made Frankie wish, not for the first time, that she was less inhibited, that she had come on to Ned a bit more before Alice got her clutches on him.

But she knew it would never happen.

'What do you make of Henry?' Nick whispered to her as they queued for burgers later on. 'I can't stand him but Mia seems to . . .' He hesitated. 'But then, she gets on with everyone, doesn't she? It doesn't mean anything.'

He looked at her, desperate for confirmation.

'She adores you,' Frankie cut in quickly. 'She's just having fun, I guess – and you know Lulu has been handing out vodka and God knows what else. Have you had some?'

Nick looked embarrassed. 'A bit,' he acknowledged, 'but I'm not good with drink and so I chucked most of it away. You know something? I drank sparkling elderflower instead of champagne at my own party.' He pulled a face. 'Don't say anything – people will think I'm a party pooper – but drink just makes me feel sick.'

'My lips are sealed,' Frankie said, smiling. 'Just go and make a fuss of Mia and tell Henry to get his fun elsewhere.'

For the rest of the evening, the band were on a high. People kept stopping to congratulate them and a couple of guys from the local radio station did an impromptu interview with Jon. After that, Jon and Jemma hung out together and although Frankie tagged along for a while, she soon got fed up of being a spare part and wandered off on her own. Around ten o'clock, she bumped into Poppy and Charlie Maddox.

'Wanna come to the Cowshed?' Poppy asked. 'There's a rave going on.'

Frankie shook her head. 'I'm just off to meet someone,' she lied.

'Hey! Who?'

Frankie gave her what she hoped was an enigmatic smile and pushed her way through the crowds. She'd had enough. The place was swarming with couples, arms linked, laughing and joking, or with groups of people, swigging lager and dancing without a care in the world.

She just didn't fit in. She was going to go home.

On the way she bumped into Nick, standing by the comedy arena entrance and looking bewildered.

'Have you seen Mia?' he asked. 'She went to the ladies ages ago and told me to wait here.'

Frankie shook her head. 'The queue is massive, though,' she said. 'She'll be back any minute, I'm sure.'

'You going to stay and watch?' he asked, and she thought she detected a note of hope in his voice. 'Can I buy you a drink?' He nodded towards the bar.

She shook her head. 'Sorry, but I'm exhausted,' she told him. 'Enjoy!'

She was almost at the exit gate when she realised that she had left her camera in the changing tent. She'd given it to Jon to take out the memory card; and then in all the excitement, she'd forgotten to pick it up. Now that the New Talent acts had finished, the flaps of the tent were closed and she was worried that her camera might have ended up in Lost Property, which was way over the other side of the site. Worse still, it might have been stolen. She loosened the ties and pulled back the tent flap.

'Oh!'

The cry escaped her lips before she could control herself. Standing in the far corner of the tent were Henry and Mia. Henry's hands were inside the back of

Mia's shorts, Mia was moaning softly and their lips were locked in a passionate kiss. At the sound of Frankie's voice, they leapt apart and stared at her, Mia's face blanching with shock, Henry looking angry rather than ashamed.

For a moment, Frankie stood frozen to the spot.

'I . . . We . . . It's not how it looks,' Mia stammered.

Frankie stared at her. 'Nick's standing out there in the rain waiting for you,' she said curtly. 'You are unbelievable!' She turned and marched out of the tent.

'Frankie, wait!'

For once, she didn't do as she was told. She wanted to put as much distance between herself and those two as she possibly could.

She was almost at the back entrance to Park House, the rain getting heavier by the minute, when Henry caught up with her and grabbed her arm.

'Let go of me!' she snapped, trying to shake him off.

'No, please, wait. You forgot this.' He shoved her camera into her hand.

'Thanks,' she snapped, and shook his arm away.

'Listen, you've got it all wrong – what you saw back there – it wasn't what it seemed.'

'I know what I saw.'

'Please,' Henry said. 'At least hear me out!' He pulled her under an overhanging tree that gave a bit of shelter from the downpour.

'How could you do that to Nick?' she demanded.

'How could *I* do that?' he countered. 'Mia came on to *me* – and I mean big time.'

'Well, it didn't look like you were fighting her off,' Frankie said.

Henry held his hands up. 'I admit that for just a second or two, I did respond. I mean, what guy wouldn't? Mia's a gorgeous girl. But you have to believe me, it was only a knee-jerk reaction. Why would I go after someone who's already engaged, especially when I'm in love with someone else?'

'I didn't know you had a girlfriend.' *Poor her*, she thought.

'I didn't say I had,' he corrected her. 'I said I was in love with someone else. She's standing beside me right now.'

It took a moment for the meaning of his words to sink in and when they did, she stepped back in horror.

'Are you saying . . . ? What are you talking about? You can't —'

'Oh yes I can.' He took her hand and held it so tightly that she couldn't snatch it away. 'That day when I lost my books and you chased after me with them – that's when it started. Ask Alice. I never made a secret of it.'

Frankie's mind flashed back to Alice's words days before. 'He likes you, he told me so. What's more, I happen to know he told one of his mates that you were cute and have got a lot of untapped potential.'

'I don't . . . I mean, I can't . . . I'm not . . .'

'Hey, it's OK!' Suddenly his hands were on her shoulders and he was pulling her towards him. 'Loosen up – you don't have to play hard to get any more.'

'You arrogant —' she began, but he pressed his fingers to her lips, pulled her hard against him and began kissing her. Instinctively, she tried to pull away but as his lips met hers, his grip on her tightened and suddenly, against everything that her head was telling her, she felt herself melting into the moment. He tasted of salt mixed with candy cane, a taste that took her back at once to the end of Brighton Pier where as a child she saved up her pocket money for popcorn and sweets. His fingers threaded themselves through her sodden hair as he pushed her back against the trunk of the tree. Still kissing her, he ran one hand down her cheek and cupped her right breast in his hand.

It was when his tongue prised her lips open that sanity returned and, using all her force, she wrenched her face away and shoved him as hard as she could.

'Get off me!' she shouted. 'What the hell do you think you're doing?'

'Just showing you how much I fancy you,' he said calmly.

'Well, tough, because I don't fancy you!' she snapped back as a flash of lightning followed almost at once by a crack of thunder made her flinch.

'Oh come on,' he pleaded. 'I know you enjoyed kissing me.'

'You arrogant —'

'Is there someone else?'

The question took her aback. What could she say? The truth would mean he would ask who it was, and a lie would give him false hope.

'I thought not,' he said with a grin. 'So I'll just have to be patient and prove that I mean what I say, won't I?' He kissed her cheek briefly. 'I'd better go and check on Alice's horse,' he said. 'He hates storms and by the look of Alice half an hour ago, she'll be in no fit state to do it herself. We'll talk more tomorrow.'

'We so won't,' she said.

But he had gone.

CHAPTER 9

'You will do as I say!'
(Jane Austen, *Mansfield Park*)

FRANKIE SCOWLED AS SHE KICKED OFF HER MUD-COVERED boots, furious with herself not just for letting him kiss her, but for enjoying it as much as she had, if only for a second. But now, slinging her waterproof on the nearest hook and going through to the kitchen, she found herself imagining how Ned would hold her, how he would taste, how she would respond.

She was searching in the fridge for a smoothie when she heard raised voices coming from the sitting room.

'I am not remotely interested. I've got more important things on my mind!'

It was her uncle – but he wasn't due back for another week! Frankie pushed the kitchen door open and ventured into the hall in her bare feet.

'But, Thomas, what will people think?' Tina was

sounding agitated in the extreme.

'Frankly, anyone with half a brain will have more important things to worry about than the antics of a few empty-headed kids!' he shouted.

'But you didn't see what they did.'

In the background, Frankie could hear the signature tune for the late-night news. She edged nearer to the sitting-room door, which was open a chink.

'It wasn't Mia's fault, of course,' she heard Nerys say. 'It'll have been that Jon.'

'For the last time, woman, will you be quiet!' Thomas snapped. 'I've had a hell of a couple of weeks dealing with things that actually matter and I come home wanting a bit of peace and quiet and all you can do is witter on about some trifling band.'

'You won't like it when the neighbours talk about your daughter stripping off on TV!' Tina burst out angrily. 'Don't you get it? Topless on TV – our daughter!

'Stupid, I agree, but —'

'And what's more, the wretched voiceover man said, "Among those letting their hair and other things down at M-Brace was Mia Bertram, daughter of Thomas Bertram, the clothing magnate".'

Frankie gasped. She reckoned Thomas would be mad beyond belief.

'Are you telling me . . .?'

Another violent clap of thunder drowned out his response and a second later, Frankie's attention was diverted by the crashing of the back door followed by squeals of laughter.

'So cook me up a storm, babes!' she heard Jon say, his speech slightly slurred. 'And I'm not talking pots and pans!'

She dashed back into the kitchen, wrenching open the door to the laundry room. 'Be quiet!'

'Oooh look, it's goody-goody Frankie!' Jemma sneered. 'Are we making a noise because we're having fun? Keeping you from your beauty sleep? Not that it appears to be working!' She giggled and then hiccupped.

'I'm trying to help,' Frankie snapped. 'Your dad's home.'

'What? Now? Already?'

'Yes, and your mum's in a strop about the dance routine. It was on TV.'

'It was? Well, it's nothing to do with me. But Dad'll be furious.'

'Well, actually —'

'On TV!' Jon butted in. 'That's amazing! Hey, have you got a laptop? We can check it out.'

The back door flew open again and the others, soaked to the skin and clearly, with the exception of Nick, the worse for drink, crashed into the kitchen. Ned was propping Alice up and looked as if he could do with help remaining vertical himself and Mia was being supported by Nick, who, judging by his tight-lipped expression, was using all his energy to keep calm. Lulu was gazing adoringly at James, who was singing some raunchy song at the top of his voice while brandishing a can of Red Bull in the air.

And that was the moment when Thomas Bertram

flung open the kitchen door and Mia vomited into the sink.

Sleep was an impossibility. Frankie tossed and turned, pummelling her pillow, kicking off her duvet, switching her light on and then off, and still her mind wouldn't calm down. Two images kept playing through her imagination like a video on repeat – Henry kissing Mia and Henry kissing her. The first made her angry on Nick's behalf; the second brought up feelings and emotions of which she was both ashamed and embarrassed. Henry wasn't to be trusted – that much was certain. So why did her body respond in this totally extraordinary and unknown way? Why did she want to cry every time she thought of Ned making Alice feel the way Henry, for just a few seconds, had made her feel?

'Get a grip,' she muttered to herself, hurling one of her pillows onto the floor and turning over for the tenth time. 'Think about something else.'

But no matter how hard she tried, memories of the previous few hours refused to go away.

When her uncle had burst into the kitchen, his clothes dishevelled and travel-creased, everyone had looked horrified. He had taken in the scene, his lip curling in disgust.

'You look like a slut,' he'd snapped at Mia. 'Those are Sylvie Costi shorts – I'd recognise her trash anywhere.'

'That was my fault,' Alice had said. 'I suggested the costumes.'

'And who the hell are you?' Thomas had interrupted

as Alice swayed gently against the larder door.

'This is Alice Crawford, Dad,' Ned had said proudly. 'And this . . .'

He turned as the back door opened and Henry, shaking droplets of water from his jacket, walked in. 'Alice, your horse is going berserk, you had better sort him – Oh!' He had stopped, catching sight of Thomas and summing up the situation in an instant. 'You must be Thomas Bertram,' he had said quickly, holding out his hand. 'Henry Crawford – Charles Grant's son. Alice and I are down for the summer. Congratulations, sir, on your award. Dad was telling me about it, and what a great friend you are to him.'

Frankie had to admit that Henry could turn on the charm as easily as turning on a tap.

'Well, yes, we go back a long way, the two of us,' Thomas replied in a slightly calmer tone.

Henry raised an eyebrow at Alice and gave an almost imperceptible nod.

'It was so good of you to let me keep my horse here,' she'd said, right on cue. 'And talking of Fling, I must go and make sure he's not kicking your stable door to bits. Henry, will you come with me? You know how I hate storms.'

With that they had both turned to leave, but not before Alice had surreptitiously puckered her lips and blown a kiss in Ned's direction and Henry had brushed unnecessarily close to Frankie, touching her wrist with his fingertips.

'I'll be off too,' Lulu had muttered.

'I'll walk you home,' James had offered eagerly, taking her hand.

'You will do no such thing,' his father shouted. 'I need to talk to you – now! In my study.'

'No, Dad,' James said firmly. 'The days of you telling me what to do are over!'

For a moment the two of them stared at one another and Frankie had noticed that Thomas's hands were shaking.

'How dare you . . .' he began, but James and Lulu had gone, James slamming the door behind them.

'I despair of the lot of you.' Thomas opened the fridge door and poured himself a glass of white wine, threw it back in two gulps and refilled it.

'Hey, Dad, don't declude . . . *in*clude . . . me in shat . . . that. I didn't do anything,' Jemma protested. 'I opted out of it all way back.'

'A pity you didn't opt out of getting paralytic,' her father said. 'Bed. Now.' He paused. 'And you?' He looked directly at Jon who was edging closer to the door. 'I don't know you, do I?'

Jon held out his hand. 'Jon Yates,' he said. 'I'm a friend of James.'

'I'm surprised he's got any left,' Thomas muttered. 'So why are you here?'

'I graduated a year ago, and I'm here because he's my best mate and we go back a long way – prep school in fact. You presented me with the athletics cup, remember?'

'No,' Thomas grunted. 'Well, I guess you'd better get home too.'

'Well, actually, James said I could stay over – if that's all right with you, of course.'

It occurred to Frankie that right now Jon had better manners than her uncle.

Thomas had waved him away and Jon had tactfully left the room as Mia, groaning, dashed to the sink and threw up again.

'I'll take Mia to bed,' Nick said helpfully. 'Well, I mean – no, I didn't mean I'll take her to bed as in . . . I meant, I'll help her upstairs and . . .'

'Go home, Nick,' Thomas had said wearily. 'Mia can sort herself out.'

'Home. Yes. Good idea. Right on. On my way.' He ruffled Mia's hair. 'Sleep it off, Mimi-pops. *Hasta la vista*, as they say in Spain.'

As Nick made for the door, knocking over a chair on his way, and Mia staggered up to bed, Thomas suddenly slumped down into a chair and rested his head in his hands.

'Dad?' Ned said anxiously. 'Are you OK?'

Thomas stared at him. 'Not really,' he said, all the energy gone from his voice. 'You think you know someone . . .'

'Mia didn't mean any harm . . .'

'Oh, I'm not talking about Mia. I'm talking about . . . life, I guess. What do we really know about people? What do we really know about goes on when our back is turned?' He drained his glass and refilled it yet again.

'Has something happened, Dad?' Ned asked, glancing anxiously at the rapidly emptying bottle.

'You mean aside from you letting your sister make a fool of herself?'

'It wasn't his fault,' Frankie burst out. 'He didn't know what the girls were planning and anyway, he was just helping out playing the guitar.'

Thomas turned and looked at her in surprise. It was as though he hadn't realised she was there at all. 'You didn't get involved though, did you?' he asked.

'No, but . . .'

'You didn't dress like a slut or behave like some stupid floozy, did you?'

Frankie said nothing.

'And you respect me, don't you? Well, don't you?' There was a pleading note in his voice.

'Of course I do,' she said.

Thomas nodded. 'For all your unfortunate start in life, and the sad example of your own parents, you've got more respect for me than certain members of my own family.' He had sighed wearily and took her hand. 'You're very precious to me, Francesca. Very precious indeed.'

Frankie didn't know what to say, but of one thing she was certain. Something had happened that Thomas wasn't admitting to. Just as James had come back from Mexico somehow different to when he went, so Thomas seemed anxious, edgy and world weary – things she would never have associated with him in the past. He hadn't even seemed that bothered by Mia's behaviour, which would normally have caused him to hit the roof. She realised that whatever was on his mind, it had to be something pretty big.

'Shall I make some tea?' she offered.

'No, you go to bed, Frankie. And you, Ned. I need to be alone.'

To Frankie's surprise, when she went into the kitchen the following morning, she found Mia sitting at the breakfast table, pale-faced and with black lines under her eyes.

'I thought you'd still be in bed,' she remarked, opening a cupboard and taking out a packet of muesli. 'Want some?'

Mia groaned. 'I shall never eat or drink again. The whole evening was one huge disaster.' She eyed Frankie nervously. 'About last night. You haven't said anything to . . .'

'To Nick, the guy who adores you? No, I haven't,' she said. 'But if you've changed your mind about things, if you don't want him any more, you owe it to him to come clean.'

'I haven't! At least I don't think I have. I was drunk, and Henry came on to me. End of.'

Frankie bit her tongue. It wasn't the version that Henry had given. 'So are you going to steer clear of him? He's trouble.'

Mia nodded. 'Nick and I are off to Barbados with his family soon, anyway,' she said. 'And guess what? Nick's grandparents have invited Jemma to come along too. Their other granddaughter, Nick's cousin, will be there and they reckon Jemma will be company for her.'

'Wow! Lucky her.'

'And when we get back, Nick and I will be going to Brighton to seriously flat hunt.'

It occurred to Frankie that Mia sounded as if she were merely reeling off a list of rather boring diary dates. There was none of her usual bragging banter, and her eyes weren't smiling.

'Cool,' Frankie said encouragingly. 'You're so lucky getting a place of your own so soon.'

'Yeah.' Mia yawned. 'I guess. Except . . .'

'Except what?'

'Oh, I don't know,' Mia sighed. 'Nick and me – we've been together since we were fourteen, and everyone expected us to get married one day. I did, I really wanted to. But now . . .'

'You're having second thoughts?'

'I don't know. Some days when I'm with him it seems so right and then on others, after I've been with . . . well, other times it just seems like it's all a sham.' She nibbled on a hangnail. 'At least even Nick agrees we shouldn't get married till we've both finished uni,' she said. 'So for now I might as well just go with the flow.'

It didn't sound to Frankie like the most romantic of suggestions.

'Francesca! Can you come here for a moment?'

Frankie was crossing the hall on her way to meet Poppy and Lulu and watch The Saltshakers' lunchtime gig when her uncle called her. He beckoned her into his study and closed the door behind them.

'About William's visit,' he began.

'It is still OK?' she asked anxiously. He looked drawn and tense.

'Of course.' Thomas nodded. 'I was just thinking – we didn't celebrate your eighteenth in a big way because you were revising flat out for your A2s. It seems unfair; after all, the others all had big parties. So I thought we should celebrate it properly while William's here. Throw a party for all your friends.'

Frankie bit her lip and looked at the floor. 'But parties cost a lot of money,' she whispered.

'Don't you worry about that,' he said.

She suddenly had an idea. 'Well, would it be rude – I mean, would you mind if . . .'

'Come on, dear, spit it out!'

'Could I have the money instead? Because uni is going to be so expensive and if I had a bit of money I wouldn't need such a big loan.'

Her uncle frowned. 'What do you mean, a loan? I pay for the others and I'll do exactly the same for you.'

'Really? Oh, thank you,' she cried. 'I can't tell you what that means to me – I was really worried . . .'

'Well, there's no need for that!' Her uncle smiled. 'And about your birthday – think it over and let me know. We'll need to get a move on if we're going to organise a big bash.'

'I don't want anything like that,' she said firmly, 'but thank you – I'll think about it.'

An idea was forming in her head but this wasn't the time to mention it.

* * *

'I am so in love!' Lulu sighed, as they made their way across muddy fields to the festival again. At least today the sun was shining. 'He kissed me – twice – he is *so* fit.'

'I take it you're talking about James,' Frankie replied. 'Just be careful – he's not exactly the reliable type.'

'Honestly, Frankie, it's no wonder you're on your own,' Lulu countered. 'Sometimes you just have to throw caution to the wind and go for it.' She frowned. 'He said he'd see me around this morning. Do you think he will? I mean, he didn't set a time or anything but then again . . .'

'See what I mean about reliable?' Frankie replied. 'He's crashed out with a hangover, I guess.'

'You are such a dark horse, Frankie Price!' Poppy Grant came dashing up to them, waving her phone in the air. 'So that's who you were going to meet last night! And just how long has this been going on?' She thrust her phone under Frankie's nose. 'I suppose *you* were in on the secret,' Poppy went on, glancing at Lulu.

'In on what?' Lulu asked, peering over Frankie's shoulder and gasping at what she saw. '*FRANKIE*! Why didn't you say anything?'

Frankie didn't reply. She was staring open mouthed at the image on the screen in front of her, feeling more and more sick by the minute. It was a close up – a close up of her and Henry in full-on snogging mode. And someone had posted it on Facebook.

'So go on, tell us everything!' Poppy said.

'Shut up!' Frankie shouted, at last finding her voice. 'Did you take this? How did it get on Facebook?'

'Course I didn't,' Poppy protested. 'I was far too tied up with my own love life to worry about taking pictures of anyone else's.'

'So how . . .?'

'I dunno.' Poppy shrugged. 'People post all sorts on the festival Facebook page – I guess someone took it and thought it was a laugh.'

'Who else has seen it?' said Frankie, hot with embarrassment and humiliation.

'How should I know?' Poppy shrugged again. 'Alice, of course. Charlie.'

Frankie's heart sank. If Alice had seen it, she'd be bound to show it to Ned.

'I don't see what the problem is,' Lulu said.

'Don't tell me you've still got a thing about Ned?' Poppy said. 'Alice has got her claws into him big time. She told me that he's so besotted she can get him to do almost anything she wants.'

'She said that?' Frankie choked the words out through gritted teeth.

Poppy nodded. 'But hey, what do you care? You've got Henry.'

'I *don't* care.' She shrugged, attempting a smile. 'Ned's loss, not mine.'

She wondered whether the words sounded as hollow to her mates as they did to her.

She was on her way back to the house when she bumped into Alice, stomping across the field wearing a riding jacket, green wellies and a very sour expression.

'Hi,' Frankie murmured, steeling herself for some risqué remark about the picture. Within seconds, however, it became clear that the only thing on Alice's mind was Alice. 'I am so angry I could explode,' she said. 'I reckon Ned's taken leave of his senses.'

Frankie frowned. 'What do you mean?'

'This stupid charity! They've brainwashed him!' Alice practically spat out the words. 'You know what? He's said he can't see me today because he'll be with a load of snotty-nosed kids in the adventure zone. Can you believe it?'

'Easily,' Frankie said. 'He's passionate about these kids. Did you know some of them have been in care all their lives, moved from foster family to foster family; some have been abused, some have —'

'Don't you start!' Alice butted in. 'I know it's awful of me, and it's great that people care, but it's the last day of the festival and I wanted to spend it with Ned.'

'You could always go and help out with the kids,' Frankie suggested.

'Get real!' Alice laughed. 'And I'll tell you something else about Ned – something only I know. You mustn't let on though.'

Frankie's stomach lurched at the thought of Ned having secrets with Alice. 'What?'

'He's got this crazy idea about being a social worker!' she confided.

'Oh that,' Frankie said nonchalantly. 'I've known about that for ages.'

'Oh. Have you?' For a moment Alice looked put out.

'And I guess you said the same as me?'

'Which was?'

'That he's a complete idiot to even think of doing something so . . . so dire and dead end.'

Frankie took a deep breath. 'Actually, I told him it was a brilliant idea and that he should go for it,' she said firmly. 'I think everyone should do what fires them up.'

'But *social work*? I mean, my God, there's no money to be made doing that. And where's the kudos? "I'm a social worker" is hardly going to open doors with the people that matter, is it?'

Frankie stared at her long and hard. 'I guess,' she said calmly, 'that it depends what sort of people matter to you.'

She turned and began walking away, but Alice grabbed her arm. 'Hey, I don't want us to fall out,' she said. 'If Ned wants to be an idiot and waste his talents, it's up to him. By the way, it's great that you and Henry have got it together.'

'We haven't,' Frankie said firmly.

'Oh sure, so that photograph was just a friendly peck on the cheek . . .' Alice laughed.

'Your brother came on to me, I said I wasn't interested – end of!'

'Was that after you had snogged him senseless?' Alice teased.

'Believe what you like,' Frankie said, struggling to keep her voice level. 'I was there. You weren't.'

And with that, she turned and walked away, leaving Alice to stare after her, open mouthed.

CHAPTER 10

'There will be little rubs
and disappointments everywhere.'
(Jane Austen, *Mansfield Park*)

'JAMES, ABOUT WHAT HAPPENED IN MEXICO. WE NEED TO talk.'

It was Monday morning and Frankie was crossing the hall on her way to catch the bus into Northampton with Poppy when she heard Thomas's voice.

'Talk? What's to talk about?' she heard James say. 'You can't deny what you did, what you let happen.'

'James, you have to believe me,' her uncle replied. 'I didn't know.'

'Do you think I'm still some kid in kindergarten?' James shouted. 'You're a businessman. You tell everyone you have your finger on the pulse. You must have known.'

'Not all of it, not about the workforce,' he said.

'Not the *workforce*, Dad,' James retorted. 'The *kids*. Go on, say it. The kids working twelve-hour shifts for a pittance in the kind of conditions you wouldn't keep a dog in.'

Frankie glanced at her watch. She'd have to run if she was going to catch the bus but somehow her feet seemed rooted to the spot.

'Look, Dad. Look at these.'

'You took photos?' Thomas croaked.

'Yes I did,' James shouted, 'because I wanted to remind myself every time I was tempted to take money from you in the future just how you came by it.'

'James, it wasn't my fault – the factory manager is in charge of all the hiring and firing. I just buy in the finished product.'

'And stick a Zeppelin label or a Cheeky Cheetah logo on it and sell it at an inflated price,' James said. 'How ethical! Now if you don't mind, I'm out of here.'

'No wait,' Thomas began. 'I need to explain —'

'There's nothing more to say. I'm meeting Jon in Leicester for a jamming session,' he replied. 'I need to get my head straight and it won't happen here.'

At that moment, Frankie's phone shrilled in her bag. Grabbing it she saw Poppy's text. *Where are you? We'll miss the bus*.

She dropped the phone back in her bag, opened the front door and headed down the drive, her mind in a whirl. Was James really saying that Thomas made his money by using child labour? He wouldn't, he couldn't – surely. And yet it seemed James had proof. And judging by the way James had been behaving, whatever had happened was serious enough to hit him – who usually laughed everything off – really hard.

Thomas said he didn't know about it and she believed him – to do otherwise was unthinkable.

On Wednesday evening, Tina organised an impromptu farewell supper for Mia, Nick and Jemma before they left for the Caribbean the following day, and all the family were there – with the exception of James who was staying with Jon – along with the Rushworths, the Grants and Henry and Alice. Frankie had hoped that Poppy would come but she was at a club night in Northampton with Charlie.

'Now before we eat, if I'm not very much mistaken, there's a bit of a surprise for you all!' Thomas glanced at his watch and then pointed the remote at the TV screen on the wall. 'Just a moment or two and all will be revealed!'

Tina was busying herself passing round a tray of canapés ('All organic, no additives and the bread is gluten free and made by hand by a little man in Thornton Lacey'), Nerys was regaling anyone who would listen with the ongoing saga of her boiler and the ineptitude of every workman in a twenty-mile radius, and Frankie was doing her utmost to avoid Henry and ignore the fact that Alice was perched on the arm of the sofa, her hand curled round Ned's shoulder.

'Here we go! Quiet everyone! Just you watch this,' Thomas cried.

Everyone turned to face the huge plasma screen.

'Darling, it's just adverts,' Tina protested. 'We don't want — Oh, I see!'

There was a gasp of recognition from everyone as slow-motion footage of a cheetah running across the African savannah filled the screen.

'*When a cheetah is hungry, she moves fast. Faster than any other animal on earth.*'

The image switched to a redolent cheetah, licking its lips, stretched out under the shade of an acacia tree.

'*And when she's got what she wants, she just lies back and purrs while others . . .*' The image switched to a computer-enhanced picture of various big cats prowling and roaring and looking generally fed up. '*. . . look like losers. Cheeky, eh?*'

'Oh darling, that's —' Tina began.

'Shh!' Thomas ordered, holding up his hand.

Slowly the image of the cheetah merged into a sylph-like woman, lying on a chaise longue, stretching luxuriantly and wearing silk palazzo trousers and a blouson jacket in shades of gold and tortoiseshell.

'*Cheeky Cheetah – the label for the woman who always gets what she wants.*'

As the advert ended, a ripple of oohs and aahs and 'Well done, Thomas,' echoed round the room.

'Thank you, everyone. Not bad though I say so myself,' Thomas gloated. 'And you'll notice that my girls are all wearing items from the collection – even Frankie. We do a petite size for little people!'

Everyone laughed while Frankie squirmed, knowing

full well that the jungle print sundress showed off her freckled shoulders and in her opinion simply highlighted the fact that her bosom didn't exist.

'I'm doing fashion studies,' Alice chirruped, sidling up to Thomas. 'If you want someone with innovative ideas about future trends, then I'm willing to be your intern.'

'Really?' Thomas raised an eyebrow. 'Then come and see me when you're a little less wet behind the ears.'

The look on Alice's face gave Frankie the urge to hug her uncle.

They all sat down to eat, just as the telephone rang.

'Let it ring,' Thomas said as Tina stood up to go into the hall to answer it. 'I refuse to be interrupted while entertaining!'

This was so unlike his usual approach that Frankie wondered just what had been in the jug of Pimms served before the meal.

'You know, it's a shame you three will be in Barbados for this party of Frankie's,' Thomas said. 'I'd forgotten about that when I suggested it, but with William coming it seems the right time to have it.'

'Honestly, I don't want a party,' Frankie said hastily. 'I mean, I did when I was a kid, when it was just games and jelly and ice cream.' *Before Mum got ill and Dad disappeared and everything fell apart*, she thought. 'But now —'

'I went to one of those in London last Christmas,' Mia interrupted. 'You all dress up as cartoon characters or Disney princesses – stuff like that – and have sausage and mash and nursery food and a bouncy castle and play silly games. It can be quite a blast, actually. We ended up having jelly fights in Cornwall Gardens! You could do something like that.'

'Don't be silly, Mia,' her father said. 'She's eighteen, not five.'

'Actually,' Frankie said, taking a deep breath. 'I think that would be a great idea. Only I wouldn't just invite my mates – I'd want to have some of the KOT kids.'

Ned shot her a smile that Frankie felt all the way to her toes.

'KOT kids?' queried Thomas. 'Is this some new-fangled band?'

'No, you know, the children Ned works with. The ones he took to camp?'

Ned's eyes flicked to Frankie's. He beamed widely and she tried hard not to melt into a puddle.

'What a perfectly lovely idea!' Poppy's mother cried. 'KOT does some amazing work and you know, I've got kids in my practice who are in care and could benefit from a bit of a treat. I'd be happy to help if you'd let a few of them come along too! Of course, there's the question of CRB clearance if you're going to be hands on with the kids.'

'Got it,' Frankie said. 'From helping at Sunday School. And Ned's got it because of his work at the camp.'

'Well, it does sound rather fun! I could let you have the name of the company who hired out the carousel for Nick's party,' Verity Rushworth added.

'You could hire those costumes where people walk

around dressed up as Iggle Piggle or Peppa Pig,' Jemma suggested.

'Hopefully we could get hold of some at short notice.' Frankie smiled.

'I wish I was going to be here,' Jemma sighed. 'I could make cupcakes.'

'Oh come on,' Alice broke in. 'Barbados versus a crowd of screaming brats? No contest!'

'Well,' Thomas said, 'if it's what you really want, then go ahead! I don't know much about what Ned does in his spare time but maybe I should find out. Not that he'll have much spare time once he joins the family firm!' He guffawed with laughter and everyone smiled obligingly. Everyone except Ned and Frankie, who both suddenly took great interest in their table napkins.

They were halfway through dessert – Jemma's amazing trifle – when the phone rang again.

Tina leant across to Frankie. 'Go and answer it, darling,' she whispered. 'I get really jangly when I think someone's trying to reach us. I mean, what if James has had an accident or something?'

Frankie went through to the hall and picked up the handset. 'Park House,' she said, imitating the style of her aunts.

'May I speak to Thomas Bertram?'

'He's busy at present, may I take a message?'

'It's urgent – really urgent. This is Sidney Cutler, news editor of the *Daily Telegraph*. I assure you he'll want to take this call, whatever he's doing.'

'Hold the line, please.'

She went through to the dining room where her uncle was topping up everyone's glass. 'Uncle, there's a phonecall for you. It's the *Daily Telegraph*. They said it was really important.'

Her uncle put his glass down on the side table and stood up. 'The *Telegraph*, huh? Well, I guess I should talk to them. After all, they were the sponsors of the Fashion Awards! And of course, with honour comes responsibility.' And with that he strutted into the hall and picked up the handset.

CHAPTER 11

'She does not think evil, but she speaks it,
speaks it in playfulness; and though I know
it to be playfulness, it grieves me.'
(Jane Austen, *Mansfield Park*)

FRANKIE HADN'T TAKEN TOO MUCH NOTICE WHEN HER uncle didn't return to the table, or when Ned apologised to the guests and said his father had urgent business to deal with; she had even assumed that the door slamming and raised voices after everyone had left were due to the fact that he and Tina had both polished off a great deal of wine at dinner. She was used to her uncle's short fuse.

But even she wasn't prepared for what greeted her the following morning.

The kitchen table was littered with newspapers, her uncle was pacing backwards and forwards, shouting into his iPhone, and Tina was wringing her hands like some distraught heroine in a 1920s silent movie. Frankie hesitated in the doorway for a moment and then edged past Nerys – who was spooning dog food into bowls with rather more vigour than was necessary – opened the cupboard and took out a jar of coffee and a loaf of bread.

'Thomas, dear, you must eat!' Nerys said, as Bonnie and Bridie, the Springer Spaniels, tucked in. 'You mustn't let these scurrilous rumours —'

'Nerys, will you shut up!' Thomas wheeled round and glared at her. 'Just take your damn dogs for a walk and get out from under my feet!'

'I was only trying to help!' Nerys grabbed two dog leads from the hook on the back of the door, clicked her fingers at the spaniels and marched out of the room.

'The sooner that woman's boiler is sorted out the better it will be for all of us,' he muttered under his breath, flinging his phone onto the table. 'Engaged again!'

'Uncle, what's going on?' Frankie asked. 'What did Nerys mean?'

Thomas sighed and slumped into a chair, pushing a copy of the *Daily Telegraph* towards her, folded open at page five.

'Libel, that's what it is! Libellous muck!'

Frankie picked up the paper and read the headline.

CHEEKY CHEETAH?
CHEEKY CHEATER, MORE LIKE!
Award-winning fashion designer faces allegations of sweatshop atrocities.

Like a slow-motion action replay, Frankie recalled the conversation she had overheard between Thomas and James. Slowly, not daring to meet her uncle's gaze, she read the first few lines of the report.

> *Just days after receiving an Outstanding Achievement Award at the* Daily Telegraph *sponsored National Fashion Awards, Thomas Bertram, founder of the Zeppelin, Bertie and Cheeky Cheetah labels, faces allegations of employing child labour in Mexican* maquiladoras, *where many of his less expensive lines are manufactured. A source close to the company revealed that children as young as twelve work eleven-hour shifts and if they do not reach the manufacturing target for the day, are forced to continue without pay. If a woman becomes pregnant, she is fired; if an employee arrives fifteen minutes late for work, they have to labour for three days without pay.*

Below the text was a photograph showing several young girls bent over machines sewing jeans.

'But, Uncle, surely this is all lies,' Frankie gasped. 'You wouldn't let something like that happen!'

'I didn't know – I mean, I can hardly be held responsible for the way some Mexican freeloader runs his operation, can I?' he replied, his face more florid than ever. 'Accusing me – it's an abomination. And to think my own son . . .'

To Frankie's horror, Thomas's eyes filled with tears.

'James? You think James told the newspaper? He wouldn't . . .'

'That's what Ned keeps saying,' he replied, 'but who else could it be? He was with me in Mexico, he had a camera, he had a blazing row with me about the set-up after the factory visit and he stormed off to change his plane ticket and fly home. Of course it was him. And after all I've done for that boy. Just wait till I get my hands on him! Where is he, come to that? I sent Ned to get him ages ago.'

'I'm here.'

James stood, tousled haired and tight lipped in the doorway, with Ned right behind him.

'I didn't do it, Dad, I swear to you,' he said, swallowing hard. 'I wouldn't put the family through something like this for the world.' He took a deep breath. 'I'm sickened by the way you run things, but I wouldn't sink that low. However, I guess the bottom line is that it is, indirectly, my fault.'

Thomas strode across the kitchen, his hand raised as if he was about to lash out. James flinched.

'Dad!' Ned shouted, and Thomas let his hand drop. 'Let James explain.'

'This better be good,' his father muttered, sinking down onto the nearest chair. 'Well, get on with it.'

'I was so strung up about what I saw in Mexico – about what you put those poor kids through.'

'I've told you, I didn't know!'

'Whatever. Anyway, I told Jon about it. He wanted

to know why I was in such a foul mood. I showed him the photos and he asked if he could have some.'

'And you let him?'

'He said he wanted to use them to give him inspiration for one of the videos to go with his social justice raps on YouTube,' James replied miserably.

'So it was Jon!' Thomas stormed. 'Right – I shall sue, I shall —'

'No!' James shouted. 'I rang him this morning and he swears blind that he never intended any of this to go public. He didn't go on YouTube with it. He just talked to his godfather about the whole issue of sweatshops. Like I said, he cares about social justice.'

'So what's this got to do with anything?' Tina said.

'Just that Jon's godfather is Sidney Cutler, the news editor at the *Daily Telegraph*,' replied James. 'Jon reckons that Cutler must have slipped one of the photos into his folder while they were talking – there was quite a pile so Jon wouldn't have noticed one missing.'

'So you see, Dad, it wasn't James's fault,' Ned said.

'Of course it was his bloody fault!' Thomas roared. 'He took the photos in the first place, he discussed my business with this low-life Jon, and never once did he stop to think of the consequences.'

'Dad, I —'

'You're a waste of space, you know that?'

'Thomas! Don't say that,' Tina blurted out. 'He's said he's sorry.'

'Oh, and that makes it all right, does it?' he shouted. 'He's not satisfied with bleeding me dry financially, so he tramples my reputation into the mud as well.' He turned to his son. 'Now get out of my sight. I want you as far away from me as possible.'

The look of abject misery on James's face made Frankie want to cry. He stared at his father. 'You don't mean that.'

'Of course he doesn't, darling,' Tina assured him.

'Oh believe me, I do,' Thomas said. 'I've had it with you. You're on your own.'

'Suit yourself,' James retorted. 'If that's what you really think of me, then I'm better off without you.'

And with that, he turned and left the room, slamming the door behind him.

'I'm going after him,' Tina said. 'Thomas, there are times when I just don't understand you at all.'

Thomas spent the next few hours closeted in his study on the telephone. Frankie got the guest bedroom ready for William and tried to calm Tina, who was distraught at the fact that James had packed a bag and left the house, refusing to say where he was going or when he would be back.

'Things will calm down,' she said. 'It'll blow over.'

Tina looked at her unflinchingly. 'There's one thing I know about my husband and elder son,' she said, 'and that's that they are as stubborn as one another. Neither will give an inch.' She sighed. 'I'm worried about Thomas. This publicity is stressing him out and he does so much that's good. I don't believe he knew about these girls in the factory, do you?'

'No, I'm sure he didn't,' Frankie said. *Although*, she

thought to herself, *he should have done*. *He should have cared enough to check things out.*

'Perhaps we should make a donation to a charity out there,' Tina mused. 'Something positive to give the newspapers. Or . . .'

Suddenly Frankie had an idea. 'I'll be back,' she said to her aunt, and ran downstairs, crashing into her uncle's study without even knocking on the door. To her surprise, her uncle wasn't alone. Ned was perched on the end of the desk.

'Frankie, what on earth's the matter?' Thomas asked.

'It's about my birthday celebration —' she began.

'Not now, Frankie,' Ned interrupted. 'This is hardly the right time.'

'It's precisely the right time!' Frankie insisted. 'Listen, please. This party – the one for the KOT kids – I think we should make it as big as we can and make sure the newspapers know about it. That way, we can show them what you're really like, which is the kindest, most thoughtful man anyone could wish for.'

'You dear girl,' Thomas said softly. 'I fear it won't make much difference because the press always prefer bad news to good. They'd just say I was doing it for a bit of cheap publicity.'

'They can't,' Frankie said, 'because we'll say it was arranged before all this happened and if we take Dr Grant up on her offer of help, then we can make sure she tells the reporters that you've been planning it for ages. Even though you haven't.'

Suddenly Thomas jumped to his feet. 'Frankie, you're

amazing! Ned, you can clear it with the charity, health and safety and all that nonsense.'

'Of course.' Ned nodded. 'We could have a bouncy castle, magicians, and the Rushworths said —'

'They won't be interested.' Thomas sighed. 'I had a phone call from Seamus only an hour ago. He's furious and refusing to invest in the new project. I've told him the facts but he won't believe me.'

'So we forget the carousel.' Frankie shrugged. 'There's plenty of other things we can do.'

'Maybe Alice could sort pony rides,' Ned suggested. 'But, Dad, all this is going to cost, and we'll have to work flat out . . .'

'I don't care,' his father replied. 'Hire all the help required. I need good publicity. Besides, I want to focus now on the son who hasn't betrayed me.'

'Dad, James didn't mean —'

'Leave it, Ned. Concentrate on the party. And now I must go. Things to do, people to see.' And with that he was out of the front door and into his car.

'You're a star, Frankie,' Ned said, giving her a quick hug. 'What a mess this all is!'

Frankie nodded. 'He didn't know the way that factory was run, did he.' It was a question but she voiced it as a statement.

'No. At least, he says he didn't and I do believe him. My father may be out for maximum profit, but he would never treat people like that. The *maquiladoras* were infamous a few years ago, and even Dad admits that the workers are underpaid – but he swears he didn't know conditions were as bad as they are or about the age of some of the machinists. I just wish to God that James hadn't talked to Jon about it.' He sighed. 'The thing is, the *Telegraph* had been running pieces about injustice in employment law in the Far East and Jon thought that he'd earn Brownie points for coming up with a new angle and in return get the paper to take some of his freelance pieces on music. How naive can you get?' He paused. 'I'm worried about James. He swears he's going to stay away from the house for as long as Dad's in it. He feels utterly betrayed.'

'*He* does?'

'Yes, because Dad was so furious about the way James cheated at uni and now, as James sees it, Dad's cheating too. Cheating people out of a decent work environment, good pay – all that kind of stuff.' He paused as his mobile rang. 'Hi babe!' He turned to Frankie and mouthed, 'It's Alice', like she hadn't already worked that out for herself. 'What? Oh. You've seen it . . . What do you mean? Who should be grateful?'

He bit his lip. 'Dad didn't know. What? . . . No, I'm sorry I can't come today – I've got stuff to do. We're going to make the party for the KOT kids even bigger and that means going flat out for the next few days. Hey, why don't you come over and we'll tell you all about it?'

Another pause.

'Oh. OK, then. See ya. Bye!'

'Is everything OK?' Frankie asked sweetly, trying not to feel pleased that it obviously wasn't.

'How come Alice can be so adorable ninety per cent

of the time and then suddenly say something that makes me wonder whether it's the same person?'

'I guess we all have off days,' Frankie murmured, thinking that ninety per cent was a bit on the generous side. 'What did she say?'

'That she can't see what all the fuss is about and the Mexicans are lucky to have a job at all considering they are all . . . well, I'm not going to repeat her opinion of them.' He sighed. 'I guess it's pretty much the way she thinks about the kids I work with. You know what she said? That I was turning into a boring do-gooder and that I'd get nowhere in life if I spent all my time worrying about what she called "the dregs of society".' His face flushed and his jaw tightened. 'Anyway, enough of all that. We need to make a start on the party arrangements before William comes. I'll tell you what, why don't you drive to the station to meet him? Give him a surprise to see you behind the wheel?'

'You'd do that? You'd come with me? I mean, he's not due till six-thirty and you usually see Alice —'

'Not this evening,' he said firmly. 'This evening is all about you.'

Frankie and Ned were in the garden, deciding where the bouncy castle should go, when Henry came up the drive in his MG Midget.

'Hi, you guys!' he called. 'Surprise!'

He jumped out of the car and pulled a large bag from the passenger seat.

'I twisted the arm of the costume department at the

Royal,' he said. 'Told them about the party, the charity and all that, and they've lent us these. Mind you, if we mess them up we have to pay to get them cleaned! And they want us to put up a few posters advertising their kids' half-term shows in October.'

He pulled out a pile of costumes and held them up one by one. 'A cat – that was from *Dick Whittington* last year apparently, a clown, Bob the Builder and – heaven knows what this is?'

'Upsy Daisy,' said Frankie. 'They're great – thank you so much! Now all we have to do is find someone to wear them.'

'I'll do Bob the Builder,' Henry said at once.

'*You?*' Frankie gasped.

'Sure,' he said. 'It's your birthday party, you want it to work well for the kids – what's to argue about?'

He got back in the car and grinned up at her. 'Better get home and practise my bricklaying!' He laughed. 'See you!'

And with that he was gone.

'He's such a nice guy,' Ned commented. 'Don't you think so?'

'Mmm,' Frankie said and busied herself with folding the costumes back into their bag.

They arrived at the station ten minutes before the train was due, which was just as well because it took Frankie three attempts to reverse into the only available parking space.

'You must be so excited,' Ned said. 'How long is it

since you've seen your brother?'

'Face to face? Seven months,' she said. 'We Skype when we can but it's not the same. I can't wait. There's so much to catch up on.'

'Mmm, I guess.' Ned looked thoughtful. 'Not least about you and Henry. He's your first real boyfriend, right?'

Frankie looked at him in horror. 'He is NOT my boyfriend,' she stressed, opening the car door. 'This is all because of that wretched photo, right? He came on to me – I mean, seriously came on to me. Why won't anyone believe me?'

Ned turned and gave her a smile. 'Well, you have to admit, it didn't look much like you were fighting him off.'

Frankie swallowed hard and began walking towards the station entrance. His words echoed her own to Henry when she'd seen him kissing Mia – and they also took her straight back to the feelings that had welled up inside her when she was in Henry's arms, and to the subsequent anger she had felt – anger that she knew stemmed partly from the fact that it wasn't Ned who was holding her that way.

'I was in shock for a moment or two,' she said, knowing as she spoke how feeble the excuse sounded. 'I shoved him away and told him where to go. You have to believe me.'

'Hey, it's no skin off my nose whether you like him or not,' Ned protested.

Frankie took a deep breath. 'So, if we were an item,

you'd be cool about it?' Her voice wavered as she asked the question.

'Sure I would, silly!' He laughed. 'Me and Alice, you and Henry – it'd be kinda neat.'

It was the answer she expected but not the one she wanted to hear.

He put an arm on her shoulder. 'Listen, I'll let you into a secret,' he said. 'Henry was telling me how he feels about you, and how he doesn't get the way you come on to him one minute and then pull away the next.'

'The arrogant sod!' Frankie exploded. 'I have *never* come on to him!'

'I told him you're shy and a bit . . . well, you know . . . uptight.'

'Oh, well, thank you for nothing!' she snapped. 'I'm only *uptight*, as you call it, with people I don't want in my personal space.'

'See, Henry and Alice, they're both fun-loving, out-there kind of people.' It was as if Ned hadn't heard.

'You can say that again,' she muttered. 'So, you're still OK with Alice? Even though she is against what you want to do?'

'Hey, it's not like I'm about to marry her!' He laughed. 'And anyway, I reckon that after the party, once she's seen the kids at first hand and realised just how much help they need, she'll change her mind.'

As well as being blind, Ned was, Frankie thought, the eternal optimist.

CHAPTER 12

'I cannot think well of a man
who sports with any woman's feelings.'
(Jane Austen, *Mansfield Park*)

WITHIN TWENTY-FOUR HOURS IT WAS AS IF WILLIAM HAD never been away. He had none of Frankie's shyness and definitely none of her inhibitions; and while Frankie had expected him to be stressed and anxious about the loss of his job, he simply laughed and said that if the worst came to the worst, he could always march up and down Brighton seafront taking snaps of holidaymakers.

Frankie's misery over Ned's total lack of jealousy had disappeared the moment she saw William stepping from the train. As he had scooped her off her feet in a great bear hug, she couldn't help bursting into tears. 'I've missed you so much,' she had sobbed, laughing and crying at the same time. 'I've got so much to tell you.'

'Me too,' William had agreed. 'When we're alone.'

He had nodded discreetly towards Ned, who was standing back, watching their reunion with a thoughtful expression on his face.

Once William was settled in the front passenger seat and had told Frankie how impressed he was with her driving skills, he had turned to speak to Ned, who was sitting in the back of the car.

'I read about your father in the newspaper on the way up,' he said. 'Bit of a rough time for you all, I guess.'

Frankie had winced inwardly. William had always been direct in what he said but she thought he might have been discreet enough not to mention such a sensitive issue.

'I probably sound rude raising the subject,' William had gone on, 'but I thought it best to talk to you and get the lie of the land. If my uncle would rather I didn't hang around, in view of everything, I can easily make other arrangements.'

Frankie knew this would be far from easy and gave him an anxious glance.

'No way!' Ned had said at once and proceeded to fill him in on the party plans, the work of KOT and how brilliant he thought Frankie was to choose a charity do instead of a posh dance. When he had asked Will to take some photographs for the charity's publicity, Will began telling funny stories about photographic catastrophes onboard ship and once again, Frankie wondered how come he could be so at ease so soon.

And that's how he was all evening. He had everyone in fits of laughter, regaling them with stories of rich American ladies looking for onboard romance, and guests who complained that no one had told them there would be insects in the Amazon rainforest. Frankie was never sure how much was true and how much was embellished because her brother kept a perfectly straight face throughout. Nerys, who had greeted him very grumpily, mellowed noticeably when he admired her dogs and pleaded with her to allow him to photograph them, and Ned behaved as if they'd been mates for life, pleased at William's eagerness to learn more about KOT and to help with the party. Frankie even heard Alice, who turned up within minutes of William's arrival, murmur to Ned that she was amazed that William and Frankie were related.

As soon as she could grab a moment alone with him, Frankie asked the question that had been at the back of her mind for days. 'Will you come with me to see Mum? The doctor told me last time I went down that she's going to be moved to a halfway house in a few weeks.'

William nodded. 'They sent me an email. I was going to suggest we went and sussed out the situation.'

'I'm worried,' Frankie said.

'I know.' Will squeezed her hand. 'I feel bad that you've borne the brunt of it all and I've only seen her every six months or so. It's . . . it's easy for me, sending cards and letters, but I guess seeing her in that place . . .'

Frankie nodded. 'I've wanted her to get better for so long, and now they say she is, I'm scared. Scared she'll have another setback and we'll be back to square one. I know it's an awful thing to say but sometimes I used to put off going down to Hove because it felt as if I didn't know her any more.'

'We'll go next week and see for ourselves exactly what's happening. Then I'll have to start some serious job hunting.' William sighed. 'But don't let's think about that now. Let's just enjoy ourselves!'

'And you don't mind mucking in and helping to organise the party?' Frankie ventured. 'I mean, it's probably more of the same for you, what with all the stuff you have to get involved in on the ship.'

'It'll be great,' William replied. 'Kids I can cope with – just keep me away from sixty-year-old women who want a dance partner!'

The atmosphere of jolly family reunions was dampened the next morning. The tabloids had picked up the story of Mexican workers with one of them running the headline, *OUTSTANDING ACHIEVEMENT – AT WHAT COST?* Thomas, looking as if he hadn't slept a wink, appeared on breakfast television, promising that he would be switching his manufacture of Zeppelin jeans and Cheeky Cheetah dresses from Mexico and denying any knowledge of what he called 'those unfortunate workplace practices'. Yet again, Frankie found herself wondering how that could be, and ashamed as she was, she began to think that he must have just chosen to turn a blind eye. Facebook and Twitter both had damning postings from a variety of sources and someone had set up a campaign called *Boycott Bertie* to which hundreds had already signed up.

Thomas had telephoned early that morning, warning the family not to be seen wearing any of his Cheeky Cheetah or Zeppelin clothes.

'No chance of that,' William had joked to Ned. 'Way out of my price range!'

By Monday, the PR people at Thomas's headquarters had rolled into action. A couple of broadsheets ran a story, albeit on the inside pages, of Thomas's outrage at those within his company who had failed to alert him to the problems in Mexico.

'HEADS WILL ROLL,' SAYS FASHION CHIEF, ran one headline. (Sadly, another reminded its readers that a few years earlier, the factory in Peshawar that manufactured Bertie beachwear had been closed as a result of a major campaign by locals and aid workers.) Somehow two of the tabloids had been persuaded to report that Thomas Bertram was holding a large party for deprived children at his Northamptonshire home, '*Something,' said a source close to the family, 'that he had planned months ago and which was just one of the many unheralded charitable activities of this modest and unassuming man.*'

By Wednesday, thanks to riots on the streets of several cities and a worldwide crash in share prices, the papers had lost interest and Thomas was home and in a more relaxed frame of mind – but then another worry had reared its head.

James hadn't returned and wasn't answering his phone. No one, including Jon Yates, knew where he was. It occurred to Frankie that maybe he was lying low because of his part in what had happened.

'We should ring the police,' Tina wailed. 'If he's in London, he might have got caught up in those dreadful riots and be injured or something.'

'For God's sake, woman, get a grip!' Thomas shouted. 'Do you really think we need more publicity at a time like this? For once, James is doing what I asked – keeping out of our hair. Hopefully he's sorting out his life. Strikes me it's about bloody time.'

'But not to know where he is . . .'

'He is twenty-two – old enough to look after himself. He's probably partying somewhere or conning some other poor sods.'

'How dare you speak about your own son like that!' Tina shouted, to the amazement of everyone. 'I've rung everyone I can think of, and no one has seen him. Frankly, I don't care what you say! If he hasn't been in touch by tomorrow, I'm ringing the police whether you like it or not.'

Frankie got out her phone.

Hi James! I'm having a party on Saturday – please please come. I know things are tough and I do understand where you were coming from but it won't be the same for any of us if you are not here. Let me know asap so I can prepare a goody bag for you!!! Love Frankie

She pressed *send* and prayed that the text would get some sort of response. Sure enough, within seconds, it did.

Thanks but no thanks. I'm working on getting my head sorted. You can tell Mum I'm OK – and I'm sure Dad doesn't care either way. Have a great time. J

It wasn't what her uncle or Tina would want to hear but at least he was alive. She ran down to the sitting room and passed the message on to Thomas.

'Get his head sorted? That'll be the day!' her uncle

grunted, but she saw the look of sheer relief on his face and knew she had done the right thing.

'I reckon Alice fancies you,' Frankie told William on Thursday afternoon, while she was helping him erect a gazebo in readiness for the party. 'Maybe you should make a play for her!'

She tried to sound light-hearted but she knew her own motives. After all, Alice had said on more than one occasion that Will was fit; and if the two of them got it together, she'd be on hand to comfort Ned and maybe, just maybe . . .

'She's not my type.' William sounded almost snappy. 'I mean, I don't do those spoilt, up themselves girls – I've seen enough of them onboard ship.'

Frankie was surprised at the vehemence in his voice. Will wasn't usually the judgmental type. He grinned at her. 'However, it seems her brother is definitely *your* type!'

Before she could protest at this, he went on. 'I'd like to meet this Henry – how come he hasn't been around?'

'He's doing a placement at the theatre in Northampton,' Frankie told him, 'but he'll be here at the party. He's been really good about getting costumes.'

'See? You do like him,' William teased.

'Will you get it into your head that just because a girl says a boy has done one nice thing doesn't mean she's about to throw herself into his arms!' Frankie retorted. 'Now grab this guy rope and pull!'

* * *

'This was your best idea ever and I love you for it!'

Ned came up behind Frankie as she served popcorn to some small and rather sticky children, wrapped his arms round her and squeezed her tight.

Frankie smiled and tipped her face towards his, before realising what she was doing. Embarrassed, she turned and spooned more popcorn into the cone and handed it to a little boy who grinned as though Christmas had come early.

'Just look at the kids,' Ned said, gesturing to the bouncy castle, the giant snakes-and-ladders and the fire engine, manned by the local brigade, over which swarms of children were climbing and shouting 'Fire!' 'They're having a ball. And you have to admit Henry and your brother are doing a great job too.'

Frankie laughed. 'William was always pretty good at playing the fool,' she said, as her brother, surrounded by children, stomped around in his clown costume, tripping on his outsize feet and making his red nose spin round and round. 'But I didn't think Henry would be quite so good with kids somehow. I thought he'd be more like Alice, way out of his depth.'

'Oh come on, be fair,' Ned cut in swiftly. 'So Alice didn't want to dress up as Upsy Daisy – big deal. She's doing a great job with the pony rides and she's going to help serve the teas later. I think she's being great.'

With that, he marched off, obviously in search of this wonder woman.

To Frankie's surprise, every one of her mates had accepted the invitation (at least those that weren't away on holiday) – even people from school whom she had imagined would look down their noses at a kids' party. They had entered whole heartedly into the spirit of the afternoon, jumping with the kids on the bouncy castle and shouting in all the right places at the Punch and Judy show and the antics of the magician. Thomas had made a great show of welcoming the visiting children and got the local paper and *TV East* to photograph him handing out gifts and sweets, every inch the jovial benefactor. As soon as the press had left, he went inside and poured himself a stiff Scotch. Tina had surprised everyone by organising a princess pamper tent for the girls and was busy teasing hair and varnishing nails. And Nerys was in her element, bossing the caterers about, telling the charity workers and carers exactly how they should be doing their job and generally getting in the way wherever she went.

'This is so cool!' Poppy said as Ned ushered the children into the marquee for tea. 'Like fun without having to get hammered!'

'And a good way of forgetting that A-level results come out in two days,' Lulu groaned. 'I am so going to fail the lot.'

Her downcast expression didn't last for more than a second. 'Your brother is totally fit,' she went on. 'Totally!'

'Lulu, he's dressed as a clown – you can't tell whether he's fit or not.'

'That's where you're wrong,' Lulu argued, dodging a small boy wielding a large stick of candyfloss. 'I saw him earlier getting ready and he has gorgeous eyes and the cutest butt. Has he got a girlfriend?'

'Lulu, you're outrageous!' Frankie said, not for the first time. 'I thought it was James you were after.'

'James isn't here, William is,' Lulu reasoned. 'So? Has he?'

'If he has, he hasn't mentioned her,' Frankie said. 'But he's only here for another week or so.'

'No time to waste then,' Lulu said cheerfully. 'How do I look?'

'Aside from the butterfly face-paint, you mean?'

'Ah, I forgot about that. Oh well, I'll just have to rely on my personal allure, won't I?'

She set off for the tent, pausing only to wiggle her bum and give them a three-fingered wave. 'Watch and learn, babes!' she called. 'Watch and learn!'

Frankie was still smiling after her when a cry tore across the tent.

'AAAH! Stop it! Stop it, you hateful little urchin!'

The shriek of disgust that echoed round the marquee made Frankie spill orange juice all over the table. She spun round, straining to see what was going on. Ned was already legging it down to the far end of the tent, a look of horror on his face.

'I knew this was a crazy idea! You are so out of order, you little scumbag!' Alice had got a small boy by the collar and was dragging him out of the tent.

'Alice, no!' Ned and Frankie yelled, almost in unison. 'Leave it!'

Within seconds, Alice was cornered not only by both

of them, but by two of the care workers who had come with the charity.

'Get her out of here now.' The tone of the more senior of the two was icy, as she squatted down and comforted the tearful child. 'It's all right, Liam, it wasn't your fault.'

'It so was!' Alice snapped back. 'Just look at the state of me – he tipped his blackcurrant all over me deliberately. These trousers are ruined!'

Frankie secretly thought that anyone stupid enough to wear white silk palazzo pants to a kids' party deserved all they got, but she refrained from saying so.

'Just go, Alice.' Ned's voice was brittle. 'Now would be good.'

Alice sniffed. 'I told you Frankie's idea was a stupid one,' she muttered. 'It may be what happens in the back streets of Brighton, but I'm used to classy parties. Oh, my God, no!'

Liam, clearly traumatised by the whole thing, had just thrown up over Alice's silver pumps.

'Oh whoops,' said Frankie, suppressing a smile. 'What bad luck! You'd better go and get cleaned up.'

'Ned, come with me,' Alice ordered. 'This has like really freaked me out.'

'No,' Ned said firmly. 'I'm busy. Sort yourself out.'

'I'm totally exhausted.'

Frankie sank down onto one of the few benches that hadn't been cleared away by the hire company and yawned. They had been clearing up for three hours and every bone in her body ached.

'But it was great, wasn't it?' she asked.

'Awesome!' Henry nodded. 'So how's about we all go into Northampton and celebrate?'

'You must be joking!' Ned laughed. 'If I make it to the back door, it'll be a miracle.'

'OK, so the pub, then,' Henry said. 'I mean, come on – it's Saturday, it's only nine-thirty and —'

'I think it's a great idea,' William butted in eagerly. 'You're up for it, aren't you, Frankie?'

In reality all that Frankie wanted to do was sink into a hot bath and not move for an hour, but seeing the eager expression on her brother's face, she relented. 'Sure, it'll be fun,' she said. 'Ned?'

'OK.' He sighed. 'I'll just call Alice and see if she wants to come.' Ned paced away from them, talking quietly into his phone.

'Considering she hasn't lifted a finger to help clear up, I reckon she should pay for the first round!' Henry laughed. 'My sister makes avoiding hard work into an art form.'

Ned's voice was louder now. 'Don't be silly . . . Well, I know but . . . Frankly, you were out of order and . . . Oh, suit yourself!'

Frankie tried hard to look as if the last thing she was doing was listening in on Ned's phone call to Alice.

'She's not coming,' he said, when he'd returned to them. 'I guess I was a bit hard on her.'

'You so were not!' Frankie burst out. 'She was horrid to that little boy. By the way, have you spoken to your dad? You know, about wanting to be a social worker?'

'Give me credit for a little sense,' Ned snapped. 'With all the trouble that's going on – James disappearing, the press only now calming down a bit . . .'

'You're going to have to do it, Ned,' she said firmly. 'You can't go on doing something you hate just to avoid an argument.'

'I know, and I've decided that whatever Dad says, I'm going to change courses,' Ned replied. 'But you know, it did occur to me that perhaps I should consider working for Dad – try to change the way things are done overseas? Oh, I don't know. Let's go.'

They were on their second round of drinks and Ned was finally beginning to unwind, when Henry's phone rang.

'Hello? Oh it's you – I didn't recognise the number. What? Hang on – can't hear.' He gestured that he would be back in a minute and disappeared outside the pub.

Within seconds, Frankie's phone bleeped with a text.

Well, thank you for not telling me. Your idea of a joke, was it? That was so not on. Lulu.

Frankie peered at the screen and reread the message.

What are you on about? she texted back.

'Problem?' William asked anxiously as Frankie's brow puckered in a frown.

She shrugged. 'It's Lulu. Apparently I've not told her something I should have done – and I don't have the faintest idea what she's talking about.'

'Ah.' William took a long draught of his beer, wiped his mouth with the back of his hand and shifted in his seat. 'I think maybe . . .' he began, but just then Henry came back and sat down between the two of them.

'Sorry,' he said, tossing his phone onto the table. 'That was my mother. God, that woman can talk for England. Hey, look who's here!' He turned to Ned. 'Clearly, she can't keep away from you.'

Frankie glanced across the pub. Alice was elbowing her way through the clusters of drinkers, her face pale.

'Hiya!' Ned was on his feet in an instant, his smile lighting up his face. 'What can I get you?'

'Henry, you've got to come now,' Alice said. 'Mum's house has been burgled. The police are there, but Mum's in total shock. Greg's away on business and she needs us there to say what's missing from our stuff.'

Henry gasped. 'We can't go now – I've been drinking. Tell her we'll be there first thing in the morning.'

'No, Dad says he'll drive us now,' Alice insisted. 'He's outside. Come on, Mum's in such a state and besides, I need to make sure my stuff is safe.'

Frankie was so stunned that she was the last to get up from the table. Ned had dashed after Alice and Henry, with William hot on his heels. Neither her brother nor Ned seemed to have noticed but Frankie was asking herself how, if Henry was on the phone to his mum seconds before Alice arrived, she never said a word about the burglary to him? Either Alice was lying or he was. And she knew where her money would go.

It was as she stooped to pick up her jacket, which had slid to the floor, that she saw it. Henry's iPhone. He must have snatched it from the table and missed his pocket as he dashed after his sister.

She picked it up. Slowly, and knowing that she shouldn't be doing it, she slid the bar to unlock. Glancing over her shoulder, she pressed *recent calls*.

Mia. Mia. Mia. Mia.

The last six incoming calls were from her cousin. Chewing her lip, she checked the outgoing calls.

Mia, Mia, Frankie, Mia, Mia, Frankie, Alice, Mia, Mia.

She knew she had to get the phone back to Henry. With everything that was going on, he'd need it and, whatever she thought of him, she couldn't let him leave until she had given it back.

She ran from the pub and into the lane that led to The Old Parsonage. As she ran, the phone bleeped. Maybe Henry was ringing in the hope of finding it.

It was a text.

You have to help me. I can't do this. I so want you. And only you. Mia

CHAPTER 13

'There never were two people more dissimilar.
We have not one taste in common.'
(Jane Austen, *Mansfield Park*)

'YOU MUST BE JOKING!' SAID FRANKIE. 'SO THAT'S WHY you sent me that weird text on Saturday night.'

She and Lulu were walking to school to pick up their results when Lulu dropped her bombshell.

'Am I likely to joke about something like that?' Lulu demanded. 'Are you honestly telling me you didn't know?'

'Of course I didn't,' Frankie replied, 'and I still think you've got it wrong. I mean, not every guy on earth is going to fall at your feet.'

'OK, think what you like,' Lulu said. 'Ask him. Why don't you?'

'I can't just come out with something like that – what if . . .?'

'He's your brother, for God's sake,' Lulu replied. 'I mean, you wouldn't care, would you?'

'Of course not,' Frankie said. 'OK, I'll ask him while we're away.'

'Away?'

'We're going to Sussex to see Mum.'

'Oh, and when were you going to tell your best friend about this?' Lulu sighed. 'Honestly, Frankie, it's like you're on another planet.'

'I know, I'm sorry,' Frankie said. 'It's just that something happened and I know about it – and I don't know if I should tell anyone or not.'

'Details,' demanded Lulu. 'I need details.'

'It's about Henry and Mia . . .' she began and proceeded to fill Lulu in on the details.

'Say nothing,' Lulu said when she'd finished. 'Firstly, Mia was probably drunk, or she'd had a row with Nick; secondly, chances are Henry won't be back and they won't see each other again and thirdly . . .' She hesitated, looking critically at Frankie.

'Thirdly?'

'It's none of your business.'

'But it is, because if Mia's cheating on Nick . . .'

'That's between the two of them,' Lulu said emphatically. 'It's not like they're married yet. And let's face it, you read messages that weren't meant for you and you don't have a clue how Henry would have responded. He might have told her to get lost.'

'Like pigs might fly!' Frankie retorted as they walked across the school forecourt. 'But OK. I won't say a word. You could be right.'

She didn't believe that for one moment, but nothing mattered now apart from the noticeboard in front of them.

'It's not the end of the world,' Frankie found herself saying. 'You can do retakes.'

'You don't get it, do you?' Lulu snapped. 'My dad will go ballistic. I was predicted three Bs and he thought that was bad enough, but a C and two Ds . . .' She burst into tears.

'I wish I could stay,' Frankie said anxiously, glancing at her watch, 'but I've got to go – our train leaves in just over an hour. Will you be OK?'

'I will when I've drowned my sorrows in a bottle of voddie.'

'Lulu, no!'

'I was joking.' Lulu sighed. 'Just go and have fun. And well done, by the way.'

'So isn't that good news?'

The psychiatric nurse beamed at Frankie and William.

'Yes,' Frankie said hesitantly. 'I mean, it was great when Mum rang to say she is well enough to leave, but what we wanted to ask you was . . . well, will she . . . I mean, there was that time . . .'

'As we've told you, she's very much better. You have to understand that medication has moved on as well,' the nurse said. 'Everyone is delighted with her progress. There are four flats in the block and a warden to keep an eye out and help if things get too much. She'll be just fine.'

Certainly Ruth seemed better than she had in years. She was over the moon at Frankie's A-level results, asked lots of questions about what they'd been doing, teased them about their love lives which they both insisted didn't exist, and wanted to know all about the ship that William was on. They had agreed to say nothing about William losing his job, but she amazed them by saying that she'd read in the newspapers that P&O were buying Siren Lines, and asking how that would affect William.

'It might be the right time for you to look for another job,' she suggested, and then laughed when they both stared at her open-mouthed.

'I still have a brain, darlings.' She smiled. 'I'm much calmer, much more focused. Things are really looking up. It's going to be just fine.'

'You know Mum asked whether you had a girlfriend?' Frankie ventured as they sat outside a pavement café in Church Road eating fish and chips.

'Mmm,' William grunted.

'Well, I know you haven't got one,' Frankie said, taking a deep breath, 'but have you got a boyfriend?'

Colour swamped William's cheeks. 'How did you know?'

'I didn't,' Frankie said. 'Lulu hinted at it.'

William nodded slowly. 'She came on to me and I guess I handled it badly.' He sighed. 'I said I wasn't in the market for a girlfriend and she asked if I was gay. I didn't deny it.'

'Which explains why you got stroppy when I said Alice fancied you.'

'Yes.' He nodded again. 'I'm not in a relationship – I was but it didn't go anywhere – and I was afraid you'd be uncomfortable about it.'

'Don't be daft,' Frankie replied. 'You're my brother. I love and adore you. Just make sure any guy you pick up deserves you, OK?' She paused, then went on, 'So there's no one on the horizon?'

William shook his head. 'Sadly, the guy I really fancy at the moment is as straight as a die!'

'Someone on the ship?'

'No, silly!' William laughed. 'Henry Crawford.'

It was several minutes before Frankie stopped choking on her chips.

They took a walk along the seafront and were on the pier where William was taking some moody shots of waves when his phone rang.

'Hello? Henry?'

Frankie's eyes widened and every fibre of her body went on red alert.

'How's things at your house? Really? That's the pits. And your mum? I bet she's devastated.' He pulled a face at Frankie.

'Pardon? Yes, that's right. We're in Sussex, visiting Mum . . . There is? Hang on, let me grab a pen.'

He flapped at Frankie who tossed him a Biro. He listened intently.

'That sounds perfect. So it's recruitandclick.com? That's amazing – it's so kind of you to . . . Yes, I will. Of course I will. Frankie? Yeah, she's right here. I'll hand you over.'

Frankie shook her head furiously.

'Oh, sorry, you're breaking up. I'm losing the signal.' He zapped the phone and glared at Frankie. 'What was all that about?'

'I could ask you the same thing.'

'He's seen a job advertised and he thought of me, which frankly I think is pretty decent of him, considering how stressed he must be with the burglary and everything.'

Frankie felt firmly put in her place. 'Have they lost a lot of stuff?'

'Yes, loads of jewellery, a laptop, and they stole the car too. Their mum had left the keys on the kitchen table. Henry said she might as well have written them an invitation.'

'Still, at least no one got beaten up or anything,' Frankie reasoned.

'True,' William agreed. He waved the piece of paper in her face. 'And guess what? Neptune's are advertising for trainee photographers.'

'Neptune's?'

'Just the largest onboard photo concessionaire in the world!' he enthused. 'They place photographers on loads of different ships – Cunard, Royal Carib, Norwegian, all sorts. If I could get this it would be just perfect!'

'So go for it!'

‘I will! Do you mind if we go to an internet café and download the application form?’ he asked.

‘Of course not,’ she replied. ‘I could do with a coffee anyway.’

‘You know the best thing about Neptune’s? They also place people with tour companies like Adventure Seekers and New Frontiers; you go out and photograph locations like the Amazon Basin and the Thar Desert, and when I’ve got more experience that’s just what I want to do! Isn’t Henry amazing to think of me?’

Early that evening, Frankie left her brother busily filling in the application form in the internet café and walked back along the seafront to the hospital. On the way she turned up Westbourne Villas and stood outside number 154, gazing at the whitewashed house with its big bay windows and decorated porch. The only thing that distinguished it from other houses in the road was the discreet brass plate which read *NHS Brighton and Hove City Primary Care Trust – Myrtle House*.

She hoped her mother would be safe there, would settle in and eventually be considered fully recovered and able to live in her own place. To her shame, Frankie hoped that wouldn’t happen too soon, just in case her mum expected her to move back too.

She arrived at the hospital just as the residents were finishing supper.

‘My goodness!’ One of the nurses smiled. ‘Your mum’s in luck today. One visitor after another – your friend’s with her now, in the green sitting room. It’s down there on the left, just past the TV lounge.'

Puzzled, she hurried down the corridor and into the lounge, lit by shafts of the early evening sun.

'There she is!'

She wheeled round at the sound of an all-too-familiar voice.

Sitting in one of the faded armchairs, looking totally at ease, was Henry.

'What the hell are you doing here? You're supposed to be helping your mum out!' Frankie knew she sounded rude but she didn't care.

'The police have got all the info they need, Alice is with Mum and I wanted to see you.'

'You're a dark horse, Francesca Price!' her mother said, smiling widely. 'Pretending you didn't have a boyfriend.'

'I don't,' Frankie said. 'Henry's just a – friend.'

'And I must be going,' he said hastily. 'Give you some time alone with your mum. I'll wait for you outside, yeah?'

'No.'

'She does love to tease me!' He grinned at Ruth. 'That's one of the things I adore about her.'

Frankie spent as long as she possibly could with her mother, most of it trying to convince her that Henry was the last guy on earth she would ever want to go out with. But eventually the staff came round with hot drinks and medication and she knew she had to leave. She had already had two texts from William asking if she was *still* at the hospital, and, if not, where she was now and she knew he'd be itching to get her to look over his job application. Maybe, she thought, as she kissed her mother goodbye and promised to visit again really soon, Henry would have got tired of waiting.

He hadn't. 'God, how I've missed you!' he exclaimed before she had a chance to speak. 'All the time I was with Mum, I just wanted to be with you and hold you and kiss you and now I can.'

With that he wrapped his arms around her, tipped her head back and began kissing her fiercely, his hands running up and down her back until she lashed out with her left foot and kicked him in the shins.

'What the . . .?' he gasped.

'You know what? I despise you,' Frankie burst out. 'I know all about what's going on, about you and Mia.'

His hands dropped to his side and his eyes narrowed. 'What do you mean?'

'You know perfectly well what I mean,' Frankie replied. 'You dropped your phone, remember? And I brought it back – but not before I'd seen the message from Mia.'

'You read my messages?' His tone had changed from seductive chat-up to a guilty snarl. 'How dare you!'

'When the phone bleeped I thought it might be you trying to locate it,' she said.

'Have you said anything to anyone?'

She shook her head, reasoning with herself that Lulu didn't count.

'Good,' he said, 'because Mia's really gone off on one this time. I told you before she was all over me. Well, now I'm beginning to think she's a basketcase. She keeps texting and —'

'Just stop right there!' Frankie shouted. 'Your lies don't wash with me. I saw that you had made loads of calls to Mia.'

'Yeah, of course, to try to get her off my back.'

Frankie turned away in disgust. 'Henry, people don't phone Barbados six times a day just to get rid of nuisance callers. Now just leave me alone.'

'Hey, don't be like that,' he said, grabbing her arm. 'OK, I should just have ignored Mia's calls but . . . well, she sounded so upset and I thought I was doing the right thing trying to calm her down, reminding her how much Nick loves her. I'm sorry if I messed up.'

If he had stopped right there, she might, she thought later, just might have wondered whether she'd got him all wrong. Within the next five seconds she knew she'd got him completely right.

'And anyway,' he smirked, 'you owe me. Who was it who told your brother about that job advert? That deserves at least one thank-you kiss. And if he gets the job, I'll expect a lot more than a kiss!'

She had never slapped a guy before. She thought it only happened in the movies.

'You little b—!'

She didn't wait to hear his insults. Ignoring the fact that her purse was almost empty, she waved at a passing taxi and left him standing on the pavement. She was rather pleased to see that a couple of guys on the opposite side of the road were laughing their heads off.

CHAPTER 14

'Our present wretchedness.'
(Jane Austen, *Mansfield Park*)

The next ten days were horrid. Thomas was away, firstly in Mexico, then in the Far East and when he was in the UK, he stayed at the London flat and immersed himself in salvaging the reputation of his company and the manufacture of next season's lines. Although the first rush of news items had ceased, several radio programmes including *Woman's Hour* and *The Moral Maze* had picked up on the cheap labour issues in the manufacture of must-have fashion and Thomas faced some fairly vigorous questioning as well as full-on meetings with retailers anxious to disassociate themselves from his brands. To his credit, he didn't shirk any of them and even admitted that it was his son who had alerted him to the shortcomings of the Mexican contractors.

William, to his great delight, was snapped up by

Neptune's and within a week had flown to Cape Town and joined a cruise ship heading for Australia and New Zealand.

'When will I see you again?' Frankie had asked tearfully as he had hugged her goodbye.

'Tomorrow.' He laughed. 'I'll Skype. In fact, I'll Skype twice a week till I'm back.' He hugged her again. 'Thanks for being you. You know, about everything.'

The day after William left, Ned came home from KOT camp. Frankie's spirits lifted when she saw him and dropped when he announced that he would be leaving almost immediately to join Alice in Sussex.

'She's in pieces, poor thing,' he said as he packed up his car. 'Not only is she gutted about everything that was stolen, but her mum keeps having panic attacks and can't bear Alice to be out of sight, and she's missing the horse.'

He paused and eyed Frankie seriously. 'And she's pretty upset with you actually,' he said.

'With *me*? Why?'

'She thought you and Henry were really getting it together and now he's gone off on a theatre craft summer school because he says it's all off.'

'It was never on!' Frankie exploded. 'And if it had been, it would have stopped the instant I found out that he was two-timing and going behind Nick's back!'

Too late she realised she had said too much.

'Behind Nick's back? What are you on about?' Ned stood stock still, staring at her.

'Nothing.'

'Frankie, you can't say something like that and then clam up!'

'All right, you asked for it,' she replied. 'Mia and Henry – they've been texting and calling one another the whole time Mia's been away. And at the festival, I caught them snogging and —'

'You know what? I would have expected more of you than that.'

Frankie felt sick. 'What?'

'So Mia texts her friends when she's on holiday – like, don't we all? She's in Barbados, she's sailing, riding, staying at an amazing old sugar plantation – of course she's going to want the world to know.'

'No, it wasn't that kind of —'

'What is this, Frankie? Are you jealous? Is that why you're spreading stories? Because if you are, then maybe you shouldn't have led the guy on and then been so high handed with him!'

'Ned, listen, it's not like that . . .' She broke off as a horsebox turned into the drive.

'I don't have time for this,' Ned said briskly. 'I said I'd help the guys load Fling and then I'm driving to Sussex to stay with Alice's folks for a few days.' He beckoned to the driver to turn into the paddock. 'And if you say a word of all this rubbish to Nick . . .'

'As if I would!'

Ned shrugged. 'I don't know what you'd do,' he replied. 'You've changed Frankie.'

'Maybe I have,' she said, struggling to keep her voice level. 'Maybe I'm not a doormat any more.

Maybe when a guy invades my personal space – not once, but repeatedly – tells bare-faced lies and openly deceives someone like Nick, maybe it's time to tell it like it is.'

And with that, she turned and walked back to the house, stumbling slightly as the tears blurred her vision.

He hadn't even asked about her A-level results. Come to that, neither had anyone else.

As always when things went badly, Frankie immersed herself in writing. The story about Jasper that she'd started ages ago had grown into the first six chapters of a novel and although she was pretty certain it would never be good enough to send to a publisher, she just kept going, pouring all her emotion and anger and confusion into the lives of her characters, turning Jasper into Henry and Alice into a nasty piece of work called Serena and Ned . . . well, Ned became Sam who was loved and adored by Emily but who was too blind to see that he was being duped by Serena. The faster her fingers typed, the better she felt; but every time she got to the point where logic told her that the reader needed to know what was happening between Sam and Serena down in Sussex, she couldn't go there.

'Oh, it's so lovely having the young ones back in the house!' Nerys enthused the day after Mia, Jemma and Nick arrived home. 'If only James . . .'

She paused as Tina waved a hand at her.

'Don't speak about James,' she wailed. 'He rang, you know, yesterday, and when I answered, he just said

"Ma, I . . ." and hung up! I know something's wrong, I feel it in my guts.'

'Mum, don't worry. Jon's going to see him tomorrow. He'll fill us in,' said Jemma.

'Jon? He knows where James is?' Tina gasped.

'How do you know? You've been away,' Nerys probed.

'He's been in touch with me quite a bit – texts and stuff,' Jemma said, blushing slightly. 'He didn't say anything about James not being at home, just that he was hanging out with him a lot.'

'But when I phoned him, he said he didn't have a clue . . .' Tina began, and then sighed. 'I suppose he was doing what James wanted.'

'Did he mention your father's troubles?' Nerys asked.

Jemma nodded. 'Not till I came home from Barbados though,' Jemma said. 'He said that he didn't want to spoil our holiday by telling us how bad things got after we left.'

'Not that anything could have spoilt it,' Mia added, hooking her arm through Nick's and resting her head on his chest. 'We were too busy having fun!'

Well, Frankie thought, *clearly everything is OK between the two of them. Perhaps Ned was right after all – perhaps it had been just a drunken moment of madness.*

Hard as she tried, she couldn't quite convince herself.

Nick and Mia left for Brighton two days later. The Rushworths had booked them into the Hotel du Vin, and given them an eye-watering budget with strict instructions not to come home until they had found what

Verity called 'the perfect little love nest'. Apparently they had assured Mia that despite Thomas's 'shocking' behaviour, they loved and adored her and knew that she and Nick were made for one another.

Mia had seemed on edge, talking too fast and too much, telling anyone who would listen how great it was going to be and how she couldn't wait to get her own place. But twice Frankie caught her coming out of the bathroom, clearly having been crying.

'You OK?' she asked the second time.

'Why wouldn't I be?'

'Pardon me for caring.' Frankie sighed. At which point Mia burst into tears and ran into her bedroom, slamming the door behind her.

An hour later, when Nick picked her up in his car, she was wearing full make-up and a broad smile. Her eyes, however, weren't laughing.

'She's been like this for the past week,' Jemma said when Frankie caught up with her in the kitchen, early that evening. She propped open her new *Cook Caribbean* book and began chopping ginger and tossing it into a mixing bowl. 'I was saying to Jon, I reckon something's up.'

'Are you and Jon . . . you know, an item?'

Frankie couldn't help noticing that his name cropped up every few minutes in Jemma's conversation.

'Well hardly, not yet,' she said. 'Thing is, he wants to see more of me and I really like him. Only don't say anything to Dad. He still thinks Jon meant to give that photo to the journalist guy.'

She chopped faster. 'And what with things with Mia and Nick getting a bit sticky . . .'

'Sticky?'

Jemma glanced at Frankie. 'You won't say anything?'

Frankie shook her head.

'Between you and me, I think Mia wishes she hadn't got engaged. Not that she's said so, not in so many words.' She hurled some coconut flakes into the bowl. 'Two or three times I found her crying and when I asked what was wrong, she said "Everything"!'

There was so much Frankie wanted to say but remembering her promise to Ned and to Mia, she kept quiet about that. 'But she seems all over Nick – lovey dovey and everything.'

'That's just the point,' Jemma said. 'That's not Mia's style. It's like she's trying to convince herself she wants him. Which is why . . .' She hesitated.

'Go on.'

'Nothing,' Jemma said, breaking eggs into the bowl. 'By the way, I was going to ask about . . .'

She broke off as her phone shrilled.

'Hey, can you grab that?' she said. 'My hands are all covered in flour.'

Frankie fished it out of the back pocket of Jemma's jeans, and held it to Jemma's ear.

'Jon! Hi, babe, we were just talking about ya! How ya doin'?' Jemma appeared to have adopted a totally new mode of speech. 'What? Oh my God, no!' Her face blanched. 'Where is he?' She reached for a pen. 'Wait, wait – Frankie get some paper, like fast!'

Frankie, who never went anywhere without a notebook, tore out a page and thrust it at Jemma. 'University College Hospital, London.' Jemma scribbled. 'Oh-eight-four-five, one-five-five, five thousand. OK, I'll tell Mum and ring you back. Oh God, oh God!' And with that she burst into tears.

'Jem, what is it, what's happened?'

'It's James,' she sobbed. 'He's been beaten up. They say . . .' She stumbled over the words, her hands shaking. 'They say he's in a critical condition.'

The rest of the day passed in a blur. Tina sat in the kitchen, weeping and rocking backwards and forwards while Jemma rushed down to Keeper's Cottage to get Nerys, and Frankie phoned her uncle.

'I'll get to the hospital right away,' Thomas said. 'I want you to get hold of Ned.'

'I tried, but there was no reply,' Frankie said.

'Keep trying,' Thomas said. 'Where is he anyway?'

'With Alice,' Frankie told him. 'In Sussex.'

'Right,' he replied. 'Well, when you reach him tell him to go to the hospital immediately. And Frankie?'

'Yes?'

'Get in touch with Mia and then ask Nerys to drive the rest of you to London, I don't want Tina behind the wheel of a car when she's in a state, OK?'

'Of course.'

'I'll be in touch as soon as I can. I'm counting on you, Frankie. You're the only one I can trust to keep calm.'

Frankie was helping Tina load a bag into the back of

Nerys's car when her mobile rang. It was Ned. 'I'm sorry, Ned, but —' Frankie began.

'It's OK,' Ned cut in. 'I was probably a bit hard on you and I didn't mean all the things I said —'

'I wasn't talking about that,' Frankie interrupted. 'I mean I'm sorry to spoil your holiday but there's been some bad news. It's James.'

They were on the M1 when Thomas rang Frankie's mobile. The news wasn't good. James was still on the critical list and in the operating theatre.

'He tried to break up a fight,' Thomas said, his voice cracking. 'We don't know the whole story but a witness said one of the guys pulled a knife and stabbed him. If it hadn't been for Jon turning up . . .' He left the sentence unfinished.

'Ned's on his way,' Frankie said. 'He'll probably get to you before we do. But I can't reach Mia. I've left a message on her answerphone.'

'Just keep trying. We all need to be here. As soon as possible.'

If her sister was bad in a crisis, Nerys was brilliant. She had packed the car-boot with a picnic hamper stuffed with bottles of water, fruit and cheese, plus blankets and a few pillows.

'I know we've got the flat,' she had announced, 'but if any of us stay overnight at the hospital we'll want to be comfortable.'

On the way to London, both Frankie and Jemma had repeatedly tried to contact Mia but every time it went to answerphone. They tried Nick's mobile but he didn't answer either. They tried the hotel, but were told that Mr Rushworth and Miss Bertram were not in their room.

'Oh, just let them enjoy themselves while they've got the chance,' Nerys said as she dropped them off at the hospital door before hunting for a parking space. 'It's too late for them to do anything tonight anyway.'

They followed the signs to ICU where a nurse greeted them at the door.

'He's out of theatre and the operation went well,' she said. 'I can't allow all of you at the bedside at once. His mum.' She smiled at Tina. 'And maybe one more.'

'You go,' Jemma said, nodding to Frankie. 'I feel queasy just being here.'

Frankie followed Tina down the corridor and into a side ward. James was lying motionless on his back on the bed, wired up to a bleeping machine and with a drip in each arm. His head was swathed in bandages, his right eye closed and swollen and his lips bloodless. Ned was in a chair on one side, Thomas on the other.

'Oh my baby.' Tina sank down on her knees beside the bed and took James's hand.

'There's good news,' Thomas said at once. 'The internal wounds are much less than they first thought and it seems the fracture to his skull hasn't damaged his brain. God has been very good.'

His eyes filled with tears and he swallowed hard. 'I blame myself for all this,' he said. 'I have been such a stupid, short-sighted fool.'

Just then, James stirred and opened his good eye. 'Dad?'

'James,' Thomas gasped, seizing his hand. 'It's OK, we're here. We're all here.'

'Sorry, Dad.' He struggled to get the words out. 'Sorry about . . .'

'It's all right, son,' Thomas murmured. 'Everything's going to be all right.'

After a while, the nurse suggested they should leave and let James rest.

'One of you can stay with him overnight but no more,' she said firmly.

'I'll stay,' Thomas said, rubbing a hand wearily over his eyes. 'The rest of you go and get some sleep.'

As they moved out into the corridor, Frankie spotted Jemma and Nerys at the drinks machine. The guy whose arm was draped protectively round Jemma's shoulders was Jon Yates.

'Any news? How's he doing? I wanted to go in but the nurse said no more visitors. Is that bad news? Or is he sleeping?' Jon's face was etched with worry.

'He's doing OK, he's speaking,' Frankie said.

'Well, that's wonderful,' Nerys said, 'because in cases like this, you see . . .'

She was about to hold forth from the depths of her imagined medical knowledge, but Jemma burst into tears. 'Thank God!' she sobbed. 'I thought he might die. I was horrid to him before he went away and I thought I might never be able to say sorry.'

'Hey, it's OK.' Jon wrapped his arms round her, and hugged her to him.

'Oh – well now. Yes. Well.' Clearly, for the first time since James's 'little misunderstanding', Nerys Lane was lost for words.

Over breakfast at the flat the following morning Thomas, who had spent most of the night at the hospital, filled them in about the events leading up to the attack on James.

'It was Jon who told me,' he began, picking half-heartedly at a slice of toast. 'To be fair to the lad, he came clean, admitted that he had been out of order showing his godfather the photos. But much more importantly, he told me what James had been doing.'

'Which was?' Tina urged.

'What he saw in Mexico had a profound effect on him – a far deeper effect than it had on me, I'm ashamed to say,' Thomas continued. 'Once his initial anger had passed, he told Jon he was taking a whole new look at his life and was fed up with being what he called a sponger and a con artist. He bedded down in Jon's flat and started working at a soup kitchen.'

'What? *James*?' Ned blurted out.

'Yes.' Thomas nodded. 'He told Jon that I had said he had no social conscience and that he was going to prove me wrong. Well, he did that all right.' Thomas poured himself another cup of coffee and took a deep breath. 'The night of the attack he was heading to the soup kitchen when he saw a group of thugs laying into a little lad of no more than twelve. He didn't think twice – Jon was coming out of the tube station to meet up with him and do an article about the work of the charity that ran the kitchen and he says James just dashed across the road, narrowly missed being knocked down, and began shouting at the guys to lay off.'

He took a gulp of coffee.

'That's when the biggest one turned on him and pulled the knife. Jon says James fell to the ground like a stone and they all kicked him as if he was a football.'

'That's awful,' Frankie gasped. 'How can people be like that?'

'I guess it happens when society turns a blind eye,' her uncle replied. 'I'm as guilty as the next person – I should have realised what was going on in that factory, but the profits were good and that was all I cared about.'

'Don't be too hard on yourself, Dad,' Ned said gently. 'You've stopped using those people now.'

'Yes, and there will be a lot of other things I'll be stopping,' he said. 'Last night, after you'd all left, I sat a bit longer with James. He told me about this course you want to do, Ned. Family work or something?'

'We can talk about that later,' Ned said anxiously. 'It's James that matters right now.'

'Too right, and it was James who said that if I didn't listen to you I might lose —'

He broke off as Ned's phone bleeped.

'Sorry, Dad, it's a text – it might be – Oh!'

He scanned the screen, his eyes widening in disbelief.

'What is it?' his father asked.

'Oh, nothing important. Just a mate about meeting up.'

His father nodded, obviously satisfied. 'You and I need a long talk about your future,' he said, standing up. 'But just one thing – I do now realise it's your future and not mine.'

To everyone's surprise he enveloped Ned in a bear hug and then, as if embarrassed by his own show of emotion, he switched into organisational mode. 'Right, this is what I suggest we do . . .'

It was agreed that Tina and Thomas would stay at the London flat until James was well enough to leave hospital, and the others would return home.

'Will you come in my car?' Ned asked Frankie. 'There's something I need to talk to you about.'

'I'll come too,' Jemma said quickly.

'Oh no, darling, come with me,' Nerys said. 'I was going to stop by Peter Jones in Sloane Square. I thought I could buy you a little something to cheer you up.'

'OK then!' Jemma agreed at once, and Frankie saw the look of relief on Ned's face.

At first, he said very little, concentrating on negotiating the London traffic, but Frankie could tell from the way he gripped the steering wheel until his knuckles were white that he was agitated about something. She desperately wanted to tell him about her A-level results but knew that now wasn't the time.

'You were right, I was wrong,' he blurted out. 'You can say I told you so.'

'What do you mean? What's happened?'

'That text I had at breakfast,' he said. 'It was from Alice.'

'And?'

'Read it for yourself,' he said, tossing his mobile onto her lap.

Guess what? Mia's dumped Nick! And guess who for? HENRY!!! Isn't that sooo romantic? They're here now – so get back quick. Watching all this snogging is making me horny! Love you, A xxxx

Frankie stared disbelievingly at the text, reading and rereading it. It wasn't surprise at what Mia and Henry had done that stunned her; it was what Alice hadn't said.

'She hasn't asked a thing about James,' she murmured. 'And doesn't she care what Nick's going through?'

'Precisely,' Ned sighed. 'I really thought she was . . . different.'

More fool you, Frankie thought, but didn't say a word.

'Hey,' she exclaimed, 'you've taken the wrong turning.'

'No, the right one,' Ned said. 'I've got to go to Sussex and see Mia and I couldn't face it on my own. You don't mind, do you?'

'Of course not,' Frankie replied quickly. 'But what about the others? Nerys and Jemma will expect us to be at home when they get back. What will you tell them?'

'I'll think of something,' he said. 'By tonight it might just have to be the truth.'

CHAPTER 15

'Let no one presume to give the feelings of a young woman on receiving the assurance of that affection of which she has scarcely allowed herself to entertain a hope.'
(Jane Austen, *Mansfield Park*)

'What's *she* doing here?'

Alice glared at Frankie as she opened the front door of the surprisingly modest semi-detached house in East Grinstead.

'She's family, why wouldn't she be here?' Frankie had never heard Ned speak so abruptly to Alice. 'We came straight from the hospital and . . .'

He broke off at the sound of shouting from upstairs.

'But I love you! You can't do this to me!' Mia's voice rose to a high-pitched wail. 'I dumped Nick for you!'

Frankie glanced anxiously at Ned.

'Did I ask you to?' Henry's voice was cold and even.

'We had a bit of fun – I didn't think you'd be so stupid as to —'

'Me, *stupid*? Oh, so you weren't there, then?'

Ned started towards the stairs.

'Leave them,' Alice said, grabbing his arm. 'You so don't want to know.'

Ned shook her hand off and took the stairs two at a time. He was halfway up when Mia, tears streaming down her cheeks, came rushing out of one of the bedrooms.

'For God's sake get a grip, Mia,' Henry shouted, slamming the door and chasing after her across the landing.

'NED!' Mia and Henry spoke in unison.

'What the hell is going on?' Ned demanded.

Mia pushed past him and ran downstairs, stopping short at the sight of Frankie. For a second they stared at one another, and then, to Frankie's astonishment, Mia flung herself into her arms and sobbed as though her heart would break.

'Mia, what is it? What's happened?' Frankie asked.

'I can't do it, I can't be with Nick, I told him yesterday and he hates me but it's the only way because . . . because I'm in love with Henry. And . . .'

'And?'

'Nothing.'

'Oh come off it!' Henry shouted. 'Tell them – go on. Tell them your little fantasy.'

Frankie glared at him, horrified by the tone of mockery in his voice.

'I think . . . I think I'm pregnant.'

For a moment no one spoke. Then Ned took a step forward.

'But Nick . . .'

'It might not be his.'

'You mean . . . tell me you and Henry didn't . . .?'

'Only once.'

'Once is enough,' Ned muttered. 'And you two hardly know each other. And what about Nick?' His face blanched as the reality hit him. 'You mean you don't know who . . .'

'I do know that I don't want to marry Nick. I want to be with Henry.'

'And how's Nick taken all this? I mean, if you are, and it is his . . .'

'Hang on,' Alice countered. 'Why all the high drama? She can get rid of it – no one need know.'

Ned turned to face her, shaking his head. 'I don't believe you,' he said slowly. 'Don't you have any kind of morals? Whatever Mia decides, this is a big deal. And it's her decision whether she gets rid of it, as you so delicately put it. Or is life just one big game to you?'

'Oh, Ned, come off your high horse!' Alice sighed. 'It could have been us – I could be pregnant.'

Frankie felt sick. So they really had gone all the way. She wanted to cry.

'No you couldn't,' Ned replied, 'since we have never got that far in our relationship. And you know what? I'm so glad. I just wish Mia had thought twice.'

'I was drunk,' Mia confessed, pulling yet another tissue

from the box on the armchair. 'Totally hammered.'

'So,' Frankie's mind was racing. 'Are you telling me that this all happened the night of the festival?'

Mia nodded.

Frankie turned to Henry. 'The night that you told me . . .' She paused. She wouldn't even voice the words.

'Now hang on a minute,' Henry protested. 'OK, so Mia and me, we had a bit of fun, but what happened – it just made me realise I could —'

'You thought you could have what you call 'a bit of fun' with two people at the same time,' Frankie retaliated. 'You're despicable.'

'I've been such an idiot.' Mia wept as Ned drove them home. 'I shouldn't have got engaged to Nick. I didn't really love him, not properly, not like I love – *thought* I loved – Henry. And now, he says he didn't mean any of it, and what if there is a baby and I'll have to leave uni and . . .' She choked on her tears, her shoulders heaving.

'We'll sort it out,' Frankie assured her, as Ned, grim-faced and shaking slightly, opened the car door. 'Let's just get you home. And on the way, there's something we need to tell you. It's about James.'

For once, both Frankie and Ned were relieved to find that Nerys had arrived back at Park House before them. Between them, they filled her in on the events of the day and from the moment she heard what had happened with Mia, she took charge, sending Mia to have a relaxing bath, making tea for everyone, suggesting that nothing be said to Tina or Thomas while James was still ill and, most surprisingly of all, silencing Ned when he began ranting about Henry.

'It takes two, Ned,' she declared. 'There is a word called "No" and sadly Mia didn't use it. She's behaved very badly, very badly indeed.'

For a moment Nerys looked close to tears herself. 'But bless her, she has all of us and we'll get through this,' she continued, rallying in her usual fashion. 'We'll discuss it all tomorrow when everyone's had a good night's rest.'

Rest, however, didn't come easily for Frankie. Ned had told her that it was over between him and Alice.

'She didn't once ask about James,' he had said earlier that evening while Mia and Jemma were closeted in Jemma's bedroom. 'It was me who raised the subject – and you know what she said?'

Frankie waited.

'She said that in a way she was glad because maybe now I would see sense and realise what happened when you got involved with down and outs – her words, not mine! Can you believe that?'

Frankie could quite easily, but felt this was a time to hold her tongue.

'I love her – loved her – *thought* I loved her – oh, I don't know!' He had slammed his fist into his thigh. 'I'm sorry, I shouldn't be off-loading on you – you look exhausted. It's just that I always know that you'll get it, see where I'm coming from. It's like with you I don't have to make an effort.'

Tossing and turning at one in the morning, she tried to convince herself that was a compliment. Judging by the creaking floorboards in the bedroom across the landing, Ned was as restless as she was but she knew for sure that it wasn't her who was occupying his thoughts.

This is a mess but it needn't affect us. I love you and I want to be with you – you have to believe me. H xxx

Not for the first time, Frankie wondered whether Henry really did feel something for her after all. But whether he did or not, she couldn't respond – her intuition had been right all along and she knew that she would never fully trust him. She deleted the text just as she had deleted all the others that he had bombarded her with in the past week, along with emails and bouquets of flowers (one even sporting a white teddy bearing the words *You for Me* which had gone straight to the charity shop). It wasn't just the crass audacity of the guy that made her feel sick; his lack of remorse made her despise him more than she thought possible.

In some ways, Alice was even worse. The day after they fetched Mia from Sussex, she turned up at Park House, announced that she was back living with her father and asking to see Ned.

'He's out,' Frankie told her. 'I thought you two were finished.'

Alice had actually laughed. 'Oh, he said he didn't want to see me any more,' she replied, 'but I know him too well. He adores me. You watch, the instant he sees me he'll be all over me again. When's he due back?'

'I haven't a clue,' Frankie had said curtly.

'Alice! Is Henry with you?' Mia came running downstairs, hope etched all over her face. 'I need to talk to him and he's not answering his phone.'

'The only thing he wants to hear from you is that you've fixed the date for the abortion,' Alice replied.

Mia stared at her, tears welling up in her eyes. 'Get lost,' she said softly and ran back upstairs.

'So you mean – it's OK? You're not pregnant?''

Mia shook her head. 'I wish I'd done a test earlier now.' She sighed. 'But I was just so terrified of what it might show. I went to the doctor and it's OK. He says I probably missed my period because of stress and worry and the holiday and all that stuff.'

Frankie gave her a hug. 'Have you told Henry?'

'Why should I?' Mia sounded suddenly calm. 'He didn't want to know and he wasn't there for me when I needed him. He didn't love me – and I was a fool to think he did.' She took a deep breath. 'But he did me one favour,' she went on. 'He showed me that I'm not ready to commit. I treated Nick so badly, and you know what? I think deep down I was hoping he'd dump me. Then I could get the sympathy, be the victim. What a cow I've been!'

To Frankie it seemed as if the next few days were like one of those trailers they show to advertise movies – James coming home, bruised, pale and more subdued than she'd ever known him; Nick's parents closeted in the sitting room with Thomas and Tina, voices raised; Poppy dashing to the house to say that Alice and Henry were leaving and that, three cheers, they had said they would never, ever come back to Thornton Parslow as long as they lived; Ned disappearing for hours into the gazebo with his iPod and books on social welfare; and then Jon Yates arriving, ostensibly to keep James company during his convalescence, but in reality spending more time with Jemma, a circumstance that Lulu took great advantage of, visiting James every day and managing to be the first person to make him laugh out loud.

It was on one of those visits that Lulu challenged Frankie.

'What do you mean, you haven't told them?' she burst out.

'There's been so much going on, and everyone's been in such a state.'

'So? You give them a bit of good news for a change. If you won't, I will.'

'No,' Frankie said swiftly. 'I'll do it. Tonight. I promise.'

In the event, she didn't have to. That evening she heard once again the banging of the gong in the hall, and once again found that it was her uncle who was hitting it as if his life depended on it.

'I need you in the sitting room now,' he said, a ferocious frown on his face. 'I'm disappointed in you, Francesca Price.'

Frankie's heart missed a beat. What had she done?

She walked into the sitting room, and everyone was there, all staring at her.

'You dark horse!'

'You so should have told us!'

'You are amazing!'

'So this is how we have to find out, is it?' Ned said with a grin, gesturing to his laptop, open on the coffee table. 'From Facebook?'

And there it was. A posting from William which read, *My amazing incredible little sister has only just gone and got herself four A-stars at A-level. Watch out, Newcastle – she's on her way!*

Then there were hugs, and popping of champagne corks, and Tina saying that she would have to be very careful at a northern university because it was very cold up there and she would need to wrap up warmly. And then her uncle tapped his glass with his pen.

'I just want to say something,' he began, clearing his throat. 'This has been a difficult summer for all of us – and I blame myself for most of it. I've not been a good father . . .'

He broke off at the murmurs of protest.

'No, hear me out,' he said. 'I thought I was doing the right thing – making lots of money, giving you a big house, good holidays, new cars – but what I never gave any of you enough of was my time. Well, from now that's going to change.' He took a sip of champagne. 'I've had a lot of long talks with Ned and James and quizzed Jemma and Mia on what the twenty-something scene need and want and I've taken on board much of what they've said. I'm going to be launching a totally new line – FairFolk. Fairtrade, organic and made by workers in co-operatives in developing countries. It's time I put something back. And you know the best thing?' He put an arm round James's shoulder. 'James has actually asked to work with me – not *for* me, *with* me – sourcing workers, monitoring how things are done. I'm so very proud of him.'

There were more gasps and hugs and topping up of glasses.

'What about you?' Frankie murmured to Ned.

'What about him, indeed?' her uncle, his hearing as sharp as ever, replied with a grin. 'He's going to train for social work – do what he's always wanted instead of what I tried to convince him was right for him. So there we are – a new chapter for us all!'

'And for me.' Nerys, who had been unusually quiet throughout, stepped forward. 'I'm moving.'

'Moving?' Tina gasped. 'Where? Why? It's very handy having you at Keeper's Cottage.'

'I'm going down to Sussex – taking a little house in Rottingdean,' she said. 'If all goes well, the time will come when Ruth will be well enough to leave that halfway house and she will need someone to keep an eye on her. Frankie can't be doing it, she's got a future to think of. Anyway, I shall enjoy living by the sea. It will work out very well.'

This time it was the turn of the whole family to be speechless.

Newcastle is very close to Durham, and when two people are doing exactly what they've always wanted to do, it is amazing how things fall into place. At first, Frankie and Ned met up at weekends, introducing each other to their friends and exploring the two towns. Then they found a midweek meeting was necessary as well, and on a blustery November afternoon, halfway across the Millennium Bridge, Ned stopped dead in his tracks, pulled Frankie to him and kissed her passionately on the lips.

It was everything she had imagined it would be and more.

'I love you, Frankie,' he said, 'and the weird thing is, I think I always have. Could you . . . I mean, do you think you might feel . . .'

'Oh yes,' she whispered. 'But just to make sure, could you kiss me again?'

And as he did, she knew it was all right. The future was waiting, wide open, for them to walk into together.

Also in the 21st Century Austen series

What would happen if you transferred the traumas of teenage love from Jane Austen's *Sense and Sensibility* to the twenty-first century?

Will Ellie's ever-sensible attitude towards life prevent her from ever snogging the gorgeous, but somewhat reticent, Blake?

Is Abby's devil-may-care outlook destined to land her in big trouble with Hunter, who specialises in being up himself?

And what about the baby of the family, Georgie? She's a tomboy, with more male friends than anyone, and so strong-willed she,ll never take no for an answer!

'This sharp, laugh-packed take on Austen's classic story will have you grinning from ear to ear at the romantic scrapes of the three Dashwood sisters.' *Mizz*

'Blends timeless truths about human nature while tackling modern teenage problems.' *Bookfest*

What would happen if the traumas of teenage life and love from Jane Austen's *Northanger Abbey* surfaced in the twenty-first century?

Caitlin Morland has always craved excitement. So when she wins an art scholarship to Mulberry Court school, she's delighted to be befriended by the glamorous Izzy Thorpe and intriguing Summer Tilney.

As Caitlin finds herself swept up in their exotic lives, she becomes determined to uncover the secrets surrounding Summer. An invitation to join the Tilneys in Italy shows her that things are very rarely all they seem . . .

'This is a fabulous read . . .
Full of glamour, secrets and intrigue.'
Lovereading

What would happen if Jane Austen's *Emma*
was set in the twenty-first century?

Emma Woodhouse is a caring, considerate sort of girl who is well aware of her own good fortune and talent for getting the best out of other people. Which is why, when she meets someone with untapped potential, she puts all her own interests to one side and sets out to change their lives for them. Whether they like it or not.

When Emma's childhood friend, George Knightley, needs help at his family's country house hotel over the summer, she sees the perfect opportunity to improve the lot of her new friend, the shy and unfortunate Harriet Smith. But as one after another of Emma's secret schemes go horribly wrong, she finds that nothing (and no one) is ever as simple as it seems.

'Delightful . . . Rushton adroitly creates a world of tinsel celebrity and shallow self-satisfaction contrasting it with the humility needed for real self-knowledge and a truly satisfying life.'
Books for Keeps

Love, Lies and Lizzie

What would happen if the traumas of teenage life and love from Jane Austen's *Pride and Prejudice* were transferred to the twenty-first century?

When Mrs Bennet inherits enough money to move into the kind of village she has always dreamed of, her daughters find themselves swept up in a glamorous life of partying and country pursuits.

But Lizzie and her sisters soon discover that, beneath the very smart surface, lurks a web of intrigue and rivalries . . .

What would happen if Jane Austen's *Persuasion* was set in the twenty-first century?

Anna Eliot adored the gorgeous Felix Wentworth, but still called an end to their relationship. As time passes, Anna wonders if strict parents, interfering friends and misplaced loyalties had more to do with it than she wants to admit . . .

Now he's back from fighting in Afghanistan and Anna longs to rekindle their relationship – but will he give her a second chance? Or will the echoes of the past prove too difficult to overcome?

An evocative tale of the perils of listening to others, instead of your own heart.